"I've never seen you first thing in the morning."

Marni's voice softened even more. "Back then we . . . we'd never spent a full night together."

Web skimmed a whisper-light finger over her lips. "Do you know it's been fourteen years since I kissed you? Talking has seemed more important these past few days.

At the desire in his eyes, Marni felt her insides melting. "Fourteen years ago it was the other way around.

"We're older now. Maybe we've got our priorities straight . . . but I still want to kiss you."

He stroked her cheek, and Marni began to tremble. "I never could deny you when you looked at me that way," she whispered. Then their lips met. . . .

Barbara Delinsky has done it again—
written a vivid, entertaining tale about
two wonderfully involving people. "I
wanted to explore what happens when
one-time lovers meet again," Barbara
says. "And how they've been changed by
circumstances of their past." Marni and
Web evolved from there, coming to life in
this poignant and very happy love story.

Books by Barbara Delinsky

FINGER PRINTS
HARLEQUIN TEMPTATION
  4–A SPECIAL SOMETHING
17–BRONZE MYSTIQUE
41–THE FOREVER INSTINCT
65–SECRET OF THE STONE
79–CHANCES ARE
87–FIRST THINGS FIRST
98–STRAIGHT FROM THE HEART

HARLEQUIN INTRIGUE
34–THREATS AND PROMISES

These books may be available at your local bookseller.

Don't miss any of our special offers. Write to us at the
following address for information on our newest releases.

Harlequin Reader Service
901 Fuhrmann Blvd., P.O. Box 1397, Buffalo, NY   14240
Canadian address: P.O. Box 2800, Postal Station A,
5170 Yonge St., Willowdale, Ont.   M2N 6J3

First, Best and Only

BARBARA DELINSKY

Harlequin Books

TORONTO • NEW YORK • LONDON
AMSTERDAM • PARIS • SYDNEY • HAMBURG
STOCKHOLM • ATHENS • TOKYO • MILAN

Published July 1986

ISBN 0-373-25216-1

Printed in Canada

1

INSTINCT TOLD MARNI LANGE that it was wrong, but she'd long ago learned not to blindly trust her instincts. For that very reason she'd surrounded herself with the best, the brightest, the most capable vice-presidents, directors and miscellaneous other personnel to manage those ventures in which she'd invested. Now her staff was telling her something, and though she disagreed, she had to listen.

"It's a spectacular idea, Marni," Edgar Welles was saying, sitting forward with his arms on the leather conference table and his fingers interlaced. His bald head gleamed under the Tiffany lamps. "There's no doubt about it. The exposure will be marvelous."

"As vice-president of public relations, you'd be expected to say that," Marni returned dryly.

"But I agree," chimed in Anne Underwood, "and I'm the editor in chief of this new baby. I think you'd be perfect for the premier cover of *Class*. You've got the looks and the status. If we're aiming at the successful woman over thirty, you epitomize her."

"I'm barely thirty-one, and I'm not a model," Marni argued.

Cynthia Cummings, Anne's art director, joined the fray. "You may not be a model, but you do have the looks."

"I'm too short. I'm only five-five."

"And this will be a waist-up shot, so your height is irrelevant," Cynthia went on, undaunted. "You've got classic features, a flawless complexion, thick auburn hair. You're a natural for something like this. We wouldn't be suggesting you do it if that weren't true."

Anne shifted in her seat to more fully face Marni, who had opted to sit among her staff rather than in the high-backed chair at the head of the long table. "Cynthia's right. We have pretty high stakes in this, too. You may be putting up the money, but those of us at the magazine have our reputations on the line. We've already poured thousands of hours into the conception and realization of *Class*. Do you think we'd risk everything with a cover we didn't think was absolutely outstanding?"

"I'm sure you wouldn't," Marni answered quietly, then looked at Edgar. "But won't it be awfully...presumptuous...my appearing in vivid color on every newsstand in the country?"

Edgar smiled affectionately. He'd been working with Marni since she'd taken over the presidency of the Lange Corporation three years before. Personally, he'd been glad when her father had stepped down, retaining the more titular position of chairman of the board. Marni was easier to work with any day. "You've always worked hard and avoided the limelight. It's about time you sampled it."

"I don't like the limelight, Edgar. You know that."

"I know you prefer being in the background, yes. But this is something else, something new. Lange may not be a novice at publishing, but we've never dealt with fashion before. *Class* is an adventure for the publications division. It's an adventure for *all* of us. You want it to be a success, don't you?" It was a rhetorical question, needing no answer. "It's not as though you're going to give speech after speech in front of crowds of stockholders or face the harsh floodlights of the media."

"I'd almost prefer that. This seems somehow arrogant."

"You have a right to arrogance," broke in Steve O'Brien. Steve headed the publications division of the corporation, and he'd been a staunch supporter both of Marni and of *Class* from the start. "In three years you've nearly doubled our annual profit margin. *Three years*. It's remarkable."

Marni shrugged. She couldn't dispute the figures, yet she was modest about flaunting them. "It's really been more than three years, Steve. I've been working under Dad since I graduated from business school. That adds another four years to the total. He gave me a pretty free hand to do what I wanted."

"Doesn't matter," Steve said with a dismissive wave of his hand. "Three, five, seven years—you've done wonders. You've got every right to have your picture on the cover of *Class*."

"One session in a photographer's studio," Edgar coaxed before Marni could argue further. "That's all we ask. One session. Simple and painless."

She grimaced. "Painless? I *hate* being photographed."

"But you're photogenic," came the argument from Dan Sobel, *Class*'s creative director. He was a good-looking man, no doubt photogenic himself, Marni mused, though she felt no more physical attraction for him than she did for either Edgar or Steve. "You've got so much more going for you than some of the people who've been on magazine covers. Hell, look what Scavullo did with Martha Mitchell!"

Marni rolled her eyes. "Thanks."

"You know what I mean. And don't tell me *she* had any more right to be on a cover than you do."

Marni couldn't answer that one. "Okay," she said, waving her hand. "Aside from my other arguments, we're not talking Scavullo or Avedon here. We're talking Webster." She eyed Anne. "You're still convinced he's the right one?"

"Absolutely," Anne answered with a determined nod. "I've shown you his covers. We've poured over them ourselves—" her gaze swept momentarily toward Cynthia and Dan "—and compared them to other cover work. As far as I'm concerned, even if Scavullo or Avedon had been available I'd have picked Webster. He brings a freshness, a vitality to his covers. This is a man who loves women, loves working with them, loves making them look great. He has a definite way with models, and with his camera."

Marni's "Hmmph" went unnoticed as Dan spoke up in support of Anne's claim.

"We're lucky to get him, Marni. He hasn't been willing to work on a regular basis for one magazine before."

"Then why is he now?"

"Because he likes the concept of the magazine, for one thing. He's forty himself. He can identify with it."

"Just because a man reaches the age of forty doesn't mean that he tires of nubile young girls," Marni pointed out. "We all have friends whose husbands grab for their *Vogue*s and *Bazaar*s as soon as they arrive."

Dan agreed. "Yes, and I'm not saying that Webster's given up on nineteen-year-old models. But I think he understands the need for a publication like ours. From what he said, he often deals with celebrities who are totally insecure about the issue of age. They want him to make them look twenty-one. He wants to make them look damned good at whatever age they are. He claims that some of the most beautiful women he's photographed in the last few years have been in their mid-forties."

"Wonderful man," Anne said, beaming brightly.

Marni sent an amused smile in her direction. Anne was in her mid-forties and extremely attractive.

Dan continued. "I think there's more, though, at least as to why Webster is willing to work with us. When a man reaches the age of forty, he tends to take stock of his life and think about where's he's going. Brian Webster has been phenomenally successful in the past ten years, but he's done it the hard way. He didn't have a mentor, so to speak, or a sponsor. He didn't have an 'in' at any one magazine or another. He's built his reputation purely on merit, by showing his stuff and relying on its quality to draw in work. And it has. He calls his own shots, and even aside from his fashion work gets more than enough commissions for portraits of celebrities to keep him busy. But he may just be ready to consolidate his interests. Theoretically, through *Class*, his name could become as much a household word as Scavullo or Avedon. If we're successful, and *he's* successful, he could work less and do better financially than before. Besides, his first book of photographs is due out next summer. The work for it is done and that particular pressure's off. I think we lucked out and hit him at exactly the right time."

"And he's agreed to stick with us for a while?" Marni asked, then glanced from one face to another. "It was the general consensus that we have a consistent look from one issue to the next."

"We're preparing a contract," Steve put in. "Twelve issues, with options to expand on that. He says he'll sign."

Marni pressed her lips together and nodded. Her argument wasn't really with the choice of Webster as a photographer; it was with the choice of that first cover face. "Okay. So Webster's our man." Her eyes narrowed as she looked around the group again. "And since I have faith in you all and trust that you're a little more objective on the matter of this cover than I am, it looks like I'll be your guinea pig. What's the schedule?" She gave a crooked grin. "Do I have time for plastic surgery first? I could take off five pounds while I'm recuperating."

"Don't you dare!" Anne chided. "On either score." She sat back. "Once Webster's signed the contract, we'll set up an appointment. It should be within the next two weeks."

Marni took in a loud breath and studied the ceiling. "Take your time. Please."

IT WAS ACTUALLY CLOSER to three weeks before the photographer's contract had been signed and delivered and Marni was due to be photographed. She wasn't looking forward to it. That same tiny voice in the back of her mind kept screaming in protest, but the wheels were in motion. And she did trust that Edgar, Anne and company knew what they were doing.

That didn't keep her from breaking two fingernails within days of the session, or feeling that her almost shoulder-length hair had been cut a fraction of an inch too short, or watching in dire frustration while a tiny pimple worked its way to the surface of her "flawless" skin at one temple.

Mercifully, she didn't have to worry about what to wear. Marjorie Semple, the fashion director for *Class*, was taking care of that. All Marni had to do was to show up bright and early on the prescribed morning and put herself into the hands of the hairstylist, the makeup artist, the dresser, numerous other assistants and, of course, Brian Webster. Unfortunately, Edgar, Steve, Anne, Dan, Cynthia, Marjorie and a handful of others from the magazine were also planning to attend the session.

"Do you *all* have to be there?" Marni asked nervously when she spoke with Anne the day before the scheduled shoot.

"Most of us do. At least the first time. Webster knows what kind of feeling we want in this picture, but I think our presence will be a reminder to him of the investment we have in this."

"He's a professional. He knows what he's being paid for. I thought you had faith in him."

"I do," Anne responded with confidence. "Maybe what I'm trying to say is that it's good PR for us to be there."

"It may be good PR, but it's not doing anything for my peace of mind. It'll be bad enough with all of Webster's people there. With all of *you* there, I'll feel like I'm a public spectacle. My God," she muttered under her breath, "I don't know how I let myself be talked into this."

"You let yourself be talked into it because you know it's going to be a smashing success. The session itself will be a piece of cake after all the agonizing you've done about it. You've been photographed before, Marni. I've seen those shots. They were marvelous."

"A standard black-and-white publicity photo is one thing. This is different."

"It's easier. All you have to do is *be* there. Everything else will be taken care of."

They'd been through this all before, and Marni had too many other things that needed her attention to rehash old arguments. "Okay, Anne. But please. Keep the *Class* staff presence at a minimum. Edgar was going to take me to the studio, but I think I'll tell him to stay here. Steve can take me—*Class* is his special project. The last thing I need is a corporative audience."

As it happened, Steve couldn't take her, since he was flying in from meetings in Atlanta and would have to join the session when it was already underway. So Edgar swung by in the company limousine and picked her up at her Fifth Avenue co-op that Tuesday morning. She was wearing a silk blouse of a pale lavender that coordinated with the deeper lavender shade of her pencil-slim wool skirt and its matching long, oversized jacket. Over the lot she wore a chic wool topcoat that reached mid-calf and was suitably protective against the cold February air.

In a moment's impulsiveness, she'd considered showing up at the session in jeans, a sweatshirt and sneakers, with her hair unwashed and her face perfectly naked. After all, she'd never been "made over" before. But she hadn't been able to do it. For one thing, she had every intention of going to the office directly from the shoot, hence her choice of clothes. For another, she believed she had an image to uphold. Wearing jeans and a sweatshirt, as she so often did at home alone on weekends, she looked young and vulnerable. But she was thirty-one and the president of her family's corporation. Confidence had to radiate from her, as well as sophistication and maturity. True, Webster's hairstylist would probably rewash her hair and then do his own thing with it. The makeup artist would remove even those faint traces of makeup she'd applied that morning. But at least she'd walk into the studio and meet those artists for the first time looking like the successful, over-thirty businesswoman she was supposed to be.

The crosstown traffic was heavy, and the drive to the studio took longer than she'd expected. Edgar, God bless him, had his briefcase open and was reviewing spread sheets aloud. Not that it was necessary. She'd already been over the figures in question, and even if she hadn't, she was a staunch believer in the delegation of authority, as Edgar well knew. But she sensed he was trying to get her mind off the upcoming session, and though his ploy did little to salve her unease, she was grateful for the effort.

The limousine pulled to the curb outside a large, seemingly abandoned warehouse by the river on the west side of Manhattan. Dubious, Marni studied the building through the darkened window of the car.

"This is it," Edgar said. He tucked his papers inside his briefcase, then snapped it shut. "It doesn't look like much, but Brian Webster's been producing great things inside it for years." He climbed from the limousine, then put out a hand to help her.

Moments later they were walking past piles of packing crates toward a large freight elevator, which carried them up. Marni didn't waste time wondering what was on the second, third and fourth floors. She was too busy trying to imagine the scene on the fifth, which, according to the button Edgar had pressed, was where they were headed.

The door slid open. A brightly lit reception area spread before them, its white walls decorated with a modest, if well-chosen, sampling of the photographer's work. The receptionist, an exquisite young woman with raven-black hair, amber eyes and a surprisingly shy smile, immediately came forward from behind her desk and extended her hand.

"Ms Lange? I'm Angie. I hope you found us all right."

Marni shook her hand, but simply nodded, slightly awed by the young woman's raw beauty. Because of it, she was that little bit more unsettled than she might have been if Webster's receptionist had been middle-aged and frumpy. Not only was Angie tall, but she wore a black wool minidress with a high-collared, long-sleeved fuchsia blouse layered underneath, fuchsia tights and a matching belt doublelooped around her slender waist. She was a model, or a would-be model, Marni realized, and it seemed far more fitting that she should be there than Marni herself.

Angie didn't seem at all disturbed by the silence. "I think just about everyone else is here. If you'll come this way. . ."

Marni and Edgar followed her to a door, then through it into what was very obviously the studio. It was a huge room, as brightly lit as the reception area had been. It's central focus was a seamless expanse of white wall, curving from the ceiling to the floor without a break. Numerous lights, reflecting panels and other paraphernalia were scattered around the area, and at the center was a tripod and camera.

Marni absorbed all of this in a moment, for that was all the time she was given. Anne was quickly at her side, introducing her to Webster's chief assistant and to the others who'd be aiding in one way or another. Marni was beginning to feel very much like a fish in a bowl when Anne said, "Brian will be back in a minute. Angie's gone to call him down."

"Down?"

"He lives upstairs. When he saw that everything was set up here, he went back to make a few phone calls." Her gaze skipped past Marni, and she smiled. "There he is now. Come. I'll introduce you."

Marni turned obediently, but at the sight of the tall, dark-haired man approaching, her pulse tripped. A face from the past . . . yet vaguely different; she had to be imagining. But she was frozen to the spot, staring in disbelief as he drew nearer. Webster was a common name...it wouldn't be him, not *him*. But he was looking at her, too, and his eyes said she wasn't mistaken. Those blue eyes . . . she could never mistake those eyes!

Her breath was caught in her throat, and her heart began to hammer at her chest as though it were caught, trapped, locked in a place it didn't want to be. Which was exactly the way she felt herself. "Oh, no," she whispered in dismay.

Anne felt both her momentary paralysis and the ensuing trembling. "It's okay," she murmured soothingly by Marni's ear. "He may be gorgeous, but he's a nice guy to boot."

Marni barely heard her. She stared, stunned and shaken, as Brian Webster approached. His eyes were on her, as they'd been from the moment she'd turned and caught sight of him, but they held none of the shock Marni's did. He'd known, she realized. Of course. He'd known. There was only one Lange Corporation, and only one Marni Lange to go with it. But Webster? It was a common name, as was Brian. Not that it would have made a difference. Around her house he'd been referred to as "that wild kid" or simply "him." As for Marni, she'd never even known his first name. He'd been "Web" to her.

"Brian," Anne was saying brightly, "this is Marni."

He'd stopped two feet away, taking in the look in Marni's eyes, the ashen hue of her skin, her frozen stance. "I know," he said softly, his voice barely carrying over the animated chatter of the others in the room. "We've met before."

"You've met . . . but I don't understand." Anne turned confused eyes on Marni. "You didn't say . . ." Her words trailed off. She'd never seen a human being turn into a shadow before, but that was exactly what seemed to be happening. "Marni?" she asked worriedly. "Are you all right?"

It was Web who answered, his eyes still glued to Marni's. "I think she needs a minute alone." He took her arm gently, adding to Anne, "We'll be back soon. Coffee and doughnuts are on the way, so that should keep everyone satisfied until we're ready." His fingers tightened fractionally, and he led Marni back across the floor. She wasn't sure if he was afraid she'd make a scene and resist, or if he simply sensed she needed the support. As it was, she could do nothing but go along with him. Her mind was in too great a turmoil to allow for any other action.

The din of the studio died the minute Web closed the door behind them. They were in a bright hall off which no less than half a dozen doors led, but it was to the open spiral staircase that he guided her, then up through another door and into the large living room that was obviously his own. Natural light poured through skylights to give the simply but elegantly furnished room an aura of cheer, but none of that cheer seeped into Marni, who was encased in a crowding prison of memory.

He led her to a chrome-framed, cushioned chair, eased her down, then turned and headed for the bar.

Marni watched him go. He moved with the same fluidity, the same stealthy grace he'd possessed years before when she'd known him. He seemed taller, though perhaps he'd just filled out in maturity. His legs were lean and long as they'd been then, though they were sheathed in clean, stylishly stitched, button-fly jeans rather than the faded, worn denim he had once sported. The muscle-hugging T-shirt had been replaced with a more reputable chambray shirt, rolled to the elbows and open at the neck. His shoulders seemed broader, his hair definitely shorter and darker.

He'd aged well.

"I know it's a little early in the day to imbibe," he said, giving a brittle smile as he returned to her, "but I think you ought to drink this." He placed a wineglass in her shaky fingers, then watched while she took a healthy swallow of the pale amber liquid. Her eyes didn't leave his, not while she drank, nor when he crossed to the nearby sofa and sat down.

He propped his elbows on his outspread thighs and dangled his hands between his knees. "You didn't know," he stated in a very quiet voice.

Marni took another swallow of wine, then slowly shook her head.

He was grateful to see that she'd stopped shaking, and could only hope that a little more wine would restore the color to her cheeks. He sympathized with her, could understand what she was feeling. He'd been living with the same feelings for the past three months, ever since he'd first been approached by *Class*. And those feelings had only intensified when he'd learned that the editorial staff had decided to use the chief executive officer on its first cover.

He'd had the advantage that Marni hadn't, and still he was stunned seeing her, being with her after all that had happened fourteen years before.

"I'm sorry," he said, meaning it. "I thought for sure that you'd have been involved on some level when the decision was made to hire me."

"I was," Marni heard herself say. Her voice was distant, weak, and it didn't sound at all like her own. She took a deep, unsteady breath and went on, trying to sound more like the executive she was. "I've been involved with every major decision involving *Class*, including the one to hire you. But I never knew your name was Brian, and even if I had I probably would never have guessed *the* Brian Webster to be you."

His half smile was chilly. "I've come a ways since we knew each other."

"That's two of us," she murmured somberly. She looked down at her glass, looked back at Web, then finally took another swallow. Afterward she clutched the stem of the wineglass with both hands and frowned at her whitened knuckles. "I had bad vibes about this from the start. Right from the start."

"About hiring me?"

"About posing for the cover. I argued with my people for a good long time, but I've always been one to delegate authority. In the end I told myself that they were specialists and had to know what they were doing. I couldn't possibly have known who you were, but I was *still* reluctant to do it. I shouldn't have agreed." She punctuated her words with one harsh nod, then another. "I should have stuck to my guns."

There was a lengthy silence in the room. As long as Marni was thinking of business, as long as she wasn't looking at Web, she felt better. Maybe the wine had helped. Tipping her head back, she drained the glass.

"I think they're right," Web said softly.

Her head shot up and, in that instant, the fact of his identity hit her squarely in the face again. The bright blotches that had risen on her cheeks faded quickly. "You can't be serious," she whispered tremulously.

"I am." He leaned back and threw one long arm across the back of the sofa. His forearm was tanned, corded, lightly furred with hair. "You're right for the cover, Marni. I've spent a lot of time going over the concept of the magazine with your staff, and you're right for the cover. You've got the looks. You've always had the looks, only they're better now. More mature. And God knows you've got the position to back them up."

His voice took on a harder edge at the end. Marni thought she heard sarcasm in it, and she bolted to her feet.

It was a mistake. She swayed, whether from the wine or the lingering shock of seeing Web after all these years, she didn't know. But that was irrelevant; before she could utter a protest, she found herself back in the chair with her head pressed between her knees.

Web was on his haunches before her. "Deep breaths. Just relax." His large hand chafed her neck, urging the flow of blood back to her head. But the flood that came to Marni was of memories—memories of a gentler touch, of ecstasy, then of grief, utter and total. Seared by pain she hadn't known in years, she threw his hand off and pressed herself back in the chair, clutching its arms with strained fingers.

"Don't touch me," she seethed, eyes wide and wild.

Web felt as though she'd struck him, yet she looked as though she'd been struck herself. As he watched, she seemed to crumble. Her chest caved in, her shoulders hunched, and she curled her arms protectively around her stomach. She was shaking again, and it looked like she might cry. She blinked once, twice, took a slow breath, then forcibly straightened her body. Only then did she look at him again.

"You knew. I didn't, but you did. Why did you agree to this?"

"To work for *Class*? Because I think it's an idea whose time has come."

"But you had to have learned pretty quickly who the publisher was. Why did you go ahead?"

"If your father had still been at the helm, I might not have. I wouldn't have worked for him. I knew he'd been kicked upstairs, and I'd been told you ran everything, but I wasn't sure how involved he still was. For a while there I waited to get that thank-you-but-no-thank-you call, and if it had been from him I would have said the words before he did."

"He only comes in for quarterly meetings," she said, defending her father against the bitterness in Web's tone. "He isn't interested in the details of the business anymore. And even if he'd heard your name, I doubt he'd have said anything."

Web gave a harsh laugh. "Don't tell me he's forgiven and forgotten."

"Not by a long shot," she muttered, then added pointedly, "None of us has. But he wouldn't have associated that . . . that Web we once knew with Brian Webster the photographer any more than I did." Her renewed disbelief mixed with confusion. "But *you* knew, and still you went ahead. Why?"

He shrugged, but it was a studied act. "I told you, the idea was good. I felt it might be the right move for my career."

"I don't recall your being ambitious."

A muscle in his jaw flexed. "I've changed."

He'd spoken in a deep voice that held cynicism, yes, but a certain sadness, even regret as well. All of it worked its painful way through Marni's system. When she spoke, her voice was little more than a whisper. "But when you found out you'd be photographing me didn't you have second thoughts?"

"Oh, yes."

"And still you agreed to it. *Why?*"

It took him longer to answer, because he wanted to give her the truth. He felt he owed her that much. "Curiosity," he said at last.

She shook her head, unable to believe him. If he'd said "revenge" or "arrogance" or "sadism," she might have bought it, but he wouldn't have said any of those. He'd always been a charmer.

She couldn't take her eyes from his, and the longer she looked the more mired in memory she became. "This isn't going to work," she finally said in a low, shaky voice.

Web stood, feeling nearly as stiff as she looked. One part of him agreed with her, that part swamped with pain and guilt. The other part was the one that had grown over the years, that had come to accept things that couldn't be changed. He was a professional now. He had a name, a reputation and a contract. "You can't back out, Marni," he forced himself to say. "There's an entire crew out there waiting to go to work."

She eyed him defensively. "I don't care about the crew. I'll pay for the services they would have given today, and for yours. We can find another model for this cover."

"On such short notice? Not likely. And you've got a production deadline to meet."

"We're way ahead, and if necessary we'll change the schedule. I can't do this."

His eyes hardened. He wasn't sure why—yes, he'd had personal reservations when the idea had first been presented to him—but he was determined to photograph her. Oh, he'd been curious all right, curious as to what she'd be like, what she'd look like fourteen years later. He hadn't expected to feel something for her, and those feelings were so confused that he couldn't quickly sort them out. But they were there. And he *was* going to photograph her.

He wondered if it was the challenge of it, or sheer pride on his part, or even the desire for a small measure of vengeance. Marni Lange's family had treated him like scum once upon a time. He was damned if one of them, least of all Marni, would ever do it again.

"Why can't you do it?" he asked coolly.

She stared at him, amazed that he'd even have to ask. "I didn't know you'd be the photographer."

"That shouldn't bother you. You smiled plenty for me once upon a time."

She flinched, then caught herself. "That was a world away, Web."

"Brian. I'm called Brian now . . . or Mr. Webster."

"I look at you and I see Web. That's why I can't go through with this."

"Funny," he said, scratching the back of his head, another studied act, "I thought you'd be above emotionalism at this point in your life." His hand dropped to his side. "You're a powerful woman, Marni. A powerful businesswoman. You must be used to pressure, to acting under it. I'd have thought you'd be able to rise to the occasion."

He was goading her, and she knew it. "I'm a human being."

He mouthed an exaggerated "ahhhhh."

"What do you want from me?" she cried, and something in her voice tore at him quite against his will.

His gaze dropped from her drained face to her neck, her breasts, her waist, her hips. He remembered. Oh, yes, he remembered. Sweet memories made bitter by a senseless accident and the vicious indictment of a family in mourning.

But that was in the past. The present was a studio, a production crew and equipment waiting, and a magazine cover to be shot.

"I want to take your picture," he said very quietly. "I want you to pull yourself together, walk out into that studio and act like the publisher of this magazine we're trying to get off the ground. I want you to put yourself into the hands of my staff, then sit in front of my camera and work with me." His voice had grown harder again, though he barely noticed. Despite his mental preparation for this day, he was as raw, emotionally, as Marni was.

He dragged in a breath, and his jaw was tight. "I want to see if this time you'll have the guts to stand on your own two feet and see something through."

Marni's head snapped back, and her eyes widened, then grew moist. As she'd done before, though, she blinked once, then again, and the tears were gone. "You are a bastard," she whispered as she pushed herself to her feet.

"From birth," he said without pride. "But I never told you that, did I?"

"You never told me much. I don't think I realized it until now. What we had was . . . was . . ." Unable to find the right words when her thoughts were whirling, she simply closed her mouth, turned and left the room. She walked very slowly down the winding staircase, taking one step at a time, gathering her composure. He'd issued a challenge, and she was determined to meet it. He wanted a picture; he'd get a picture. She *was* the publisher of this magazine, and, yes, she was a powerful businesswoman. Web had decimated her once before. She was not going to let it happen again.

By the time she reentered the studio, she was concentrating on business, her sole source of salvation. Anne rushed to her side and studied her closely. "Are you okay?"

"I'm fine," she said.

"God, I'm sorry, Marni. I didn't realize that you knew him."

"Neither did I."

"Are you over the shock?"

"The shock, yes."

"But he's not your favorite person. You don't know how *awful* I feel. Here we've been shoving him at you—"

"But you were right, Anne. He's a superb photographer, and he's the right man for *Class*. My personal feelings are irrelevant. This is pure business." Her chin was tipped up, but Anne couldn't miss the pinched look around her mouth.

"But you didn't want to be on the cover to begin with, and now you've got to cope with Brian."

"Brian won't bother me." It was Web who would...if she let him. She simply wouldn't allow it. That was that! "I think we'd better get going. I've got piles of things waiting for me at the office."

Anne gave her a last skeptical once-over before turning and gesturing to Webster's assistant.

In the hour that followed, Marni was shuttled from side room to side room. She submitted to having her hair completely done, all the while concentrating on the meeting she would set up the next day with the management of her computer division. She watched her face as it was cleaned, then skillfully made up, but her thoughts were on a newly risen distribution problem in the medical supplies section. She let herself be stripped, then dressed, but her mind was on the possibility of luring one particularly brilliant competitor to head Lange's market research department. As a result, she was as oblivious to the vividly patterned silk shirt and blouse, to the onyx necklace, bracelet and earrings put on her as she was to the fact that the finished product was positively breathtaking.

The audience in the main room was oblivious to no such thing. The minute she stepped from the dressing room she was met by a series of "ooohs" and "ahhhs," immediately followed by a cacophony of chatter.

But she was insulated. In the time it had taken for Webster's people to make her camera-ready, she'd built a wall around herself. She was barely aware of being led to a high, backless stool set in the center of the seamless expanse of curving white wall. She was barely aware of the man who continued to poke at her hair, or the one who lightly brushed powder on her neck, throat and the narrow V between her breasts, or the woman who smoothed her skirt into gentle folds around her legs and adjusted the neckline of her blouse.

She was aware of Web, though, the minute he came to stand before her with his legs planted apart and his eyes scrutinizing what she'd become. She felt her heart beat faster, so she conjured the image of that particularly brilliant competitor she wanted to head the market research division. She'd met the man several times, yet now his image kept fading. She blinked, swallowed and tried again, this time thinking of the upcoming stockholders' meeting and the issues to be dealt with. But the issues slipped from mind. Something about rewriting bylaws...hostile takeover attempts...

Web turned to issue orders to his assistants, and she let out the breath she hadn't realized she'd been holding. A quartz floodlight was set here, another there. Reflectors were placed appropriately. A smaller spotlight was put farther to one side, another to the back, several more brought down from overhead. Web moved around her, studying her from every angle, consulting his light meter at each one.

She felt like a yo-yo, spinning to the end of its rope when he looked at her, recoiling in relief when he looked away. She didn't want to think ahead to when he'd be behind his camera focusing solely on her, for it filled her with dread. So she closed her eyes and thought yoga thoughts, blank mind, deep steady breaths, relaxation.

She'd never been all that good at yoga.

She put herself into a field of wildflowers glowing in the springtime sun. But the sun was too hot, and the wildflowers began doing something to her sinuses, not to mention her stomach. And there was a noise that should have been appropriate but somehow was grating. The chirping of birds, the trickle of a nearby stream.... No, the sounds of a gentle piano ... a lilting love song ...

Her eyes riveted to Web, who approached her barehanded. "That music," she breathed. "Is it necessary?"

He spoke as softly as she had. "I thought it might relax you, put you in the mood."

"You've got to be kidding."

"Actually, I wasn't. If it bothers you—"

"It does. I don't like it."

"Would you like something else?"

"Silence would be fine."

"I need to be put in the mood, too."

"Then put on something else," she whispered plaintively, and breathed a sigh of relief when he walked to the side to talk with one of his assistants, who promptly headed off in the other direction. Marni barely had time to register the spectators gathered in haphazard clusters beyond camera range, sipping coffee, munching doughnuts and talking among themselves as they observed the proceedings, when

Web returned. He stood very close and regarded her gently. She felt the muscles around her heart constrict.

He put his hands on her shoulders and tightened his fingers when she would have leaned back out of his grasp. "I want you to relax," he ordered very softly, his face inches above hers. He began to slowly knead the tension from her shoulders. "If we're going to get anything out of this, you've got to relax."

The background music stopped abruptly. "I can't relax when you're touching me," she whispered.

"You'll have to get used to that. I'll have to touch you, to turn you here or there where I want you."

"You can tell me what to do. You don't have to do it for me."

His hands kept up their kneading, though her muscles refused to respond. "I enjoy touching you. You're a very beautiful woman."

She closed her eyes. "Please, no. Don't play your games with me."

"I'm not playing games. I'm very serious."

"I can't take it." Just then the music began again, this time to a more popular, faster beat. Her eyes flew open. "Oh, God, you're not going to have me *move*, are you?"

He had to smile at the sheer terror in her eyes. "Would it be so awful?"

Her expression was mutinous. "I won't do that, Web. I'm not a model, or a dancer, or an exhibitionist, and I *refuse* to make an utter fool out of myself in front of all these people."

He was still smiling. At the age of thirty-one, she was more beautiful than he'd ever imagined she'd be. Though he had no right to, he felt a certain pride in her. "Take it easy, Marni. I won't make you dance. Or move. We'll just both flow with the music. How does that sound?"

It sounded awful, and his smile was upsetting her all the more. "I'm not really up for flowing."

"What are you up for?"

Her eyes widened on his face in search of smugness, but there was none. Nor had there been suggestiveness in his tone, which maintained the same soft and gentle lilt. He was trying to be understanding of her and of the situation they'd found themselves in, she realized. She also realized that there were tiny crow's-feet at either corner of his eyes and smile lines by his mouth, and that his skin had the rougher texture maturity gave a man. A thicker beard, though recently shaven, left a virile shadow around his mouth and along his jaw.

His hands on her shoulders had stopped moving. She averted her gaze to the floor. "I'm not up for much right about now, but I guess we'd better get on with this."

"A bit of pain . . . a blaze of glory?"

She jerked her eyes back to his, and quite helplessly they flooded. "How *could* you?" she whispered brokenly.

He leaned forward and pressed his lips to her damp brow, then murmured against her skin, for her ears alone, "I want you to remember, Marni. I want you to think about what we had. That first time on the shore, the other times in the woods and on my narrow little cot."

Too weak to pull away from him, and further hamstrung by the people watching, she simply closed her eyes and struggled to regain her self-control. Web drew back and brushed a tear from the corner of her eye.

"Remember it, Marni," he whispered gently. "Remember how good it was, how soft and warm and exciting. Pretend we're back there now, that we're lovers stealing away from the real world, keeping secrets only the two of us share. Pretend that there's danger, that what we're doing is slightly illicit, but that we're very, very sure of ourselves."

"But the rest—"

"Remember the good part, babe. Remember it when you look at me now. I want confidence from you. I want defiance and promise and success, and that special kind of feminine spirit that captivated me from the start. You've got it in you. Let me see it."

He stepped back then and, without another word, went to his camera.

Stunned and more confused than ever, Marni stared after him. Brushes dabbed at her cheeks and glossed her lips; fingers plucked at her hair. She wanted to push them away, because they intruded on her thoughts. But she had no more power to lift a hand than she had to get up and walk from the room as that tiny voice of instinct told her to do.

It began then. With his legs braced apart and his eyes alternating between the camera lens and her, Web gave soft commands to the lighting crew. Then, "Let's get a few straightforward shots first. Look here, Marni."

She'd been looking at him all along, watching as he peered through the lens, then stepped to the side holding the remote cord to the shutter. She felt wooden. "I don't know what to do. Am I supposed to . . . smile?"

"Just relax. Do whatever you want. Tip your head up...a little to the left . . . atta girl." Click.

Marni made no attempt to smile. She didn't want to smile. What she wanted to do was cry, but she couldn't do that.

"Run your tongue over your lips." Click. "Good. Again." Click. Click. "Shake your head . . . that's the way . . . like the ocean breeze . . . warm summer's night . . ."

Marni stared at the camera in agony, wanting to remember as he was urging but simultaneously fighting the pain.

He left the camera and came to her, shifting her on the stool, repositioning her legs, her arms, her shoulders, her head, all the time murmuring soft words of encouragement that backfired in her mind. He returned to the camera, tripped the lens twice, then lifted the tripod and moved the entire apparatus forward.

"Okay, Marni," he said, his voice modulated so that it just reached her, "now I want you to turn your face away from me. That's it. Just your head. Now close your eyes and remember what I told you. Think sand and stars and a beautiful full moon. Let the music help you." The words of a trendy pop ballad were shimmering through the room. "That's it. Now, very slowly, turn back toward me . . . open your eyes . . . a smug little smile . . ."

Marni struggled. She turned her head as he'd said. She thought of sand—she and Web lying on it—and stars and a beautiful full moon—she and Web lying beneath them— and she very slowly turned back toward him. But when she opened her eyes, they were filled with tears, and she couldn't muster even the smallest smile.

Web didn't take a shot. Patiently, he straightened, then put out a hand when Anne started toward Marni. She retreated, and Web moved forward. "Not exactly what I was looking for," he said on a wistfully teasing note.

"I'm sorry." She blinked once, twice, then she was in control again. The music had picked up, and she caught sight of feet tapping, knees bending, bodies rocking rhythmically on the sidelines. "I feel awkward."

"It's okay. We'll try again." He gestured for his aides to touch her up, then returned to stand by his camera with the remote cord in his hand. "Okay, Marni. Let your head fall back. That's it. Now concentrate on relaxing your shoulders. Riiiiight. Now bring your head back up real quick and look the camera in the eye. Good. That's my girl! Better." He advanced the film once, then again, and a third time. What he was capturing was better than what had come before, he knew, but it was nowhere near the look, the feeling he wanted.

He could have her hair fixed, or her clothes, or her makeup. He could shift her this way or that, could put her in any number of poses. But he couldn't take the pain from her eyes.

He'd told her to remember the good and the beautiful, because that was what he wanted to do himself. But she couldn't separate the good from all that had come after and, with sorrow on her face and pain in her eyes, he couldn't either.

So he took a different tack, a more businesslike one he felt would be more palatable to her. He talked to her, still softly, but of the magazine now, of the image they all wanted for it, of the success it was going to be. He posed her, coaxed her, took several shots, then frowned. He took the stool away, replaced one lens with another his assistant handed him and exposed nearly a roll of film with her standing—straight, then with her weight balanced on one hip, with her hands folded before her, one hand on her hip, one hand on each, the two clasped behind her head. When her legs began to visibly tremble, he set her back on the stool.

He changed lights, bathing the background in green, then yellow, then pale blue. He switched to a hand-held camera so that he could more freely move around, changing lenses and the angle of his shots, building a momentum in the hopes of distracting Marni from the thoughts that brought tears to her eyes every time he was on the verge of getting something good.

For Marni it was trial by fire, and she knew she was failing miserably. When Web, infuriatingly solicitous, approached her between a series of shots, she put the blame on the self-consciousness she felt, then on the heat of the lights, then on the crick in her neck. One hour became two, then three. When she began to wilt, she was whisked off for a change of clothes and a glass of orange juice, but the remedial treatment was akin to a finger in the dike. She ached from the inside out, and it was all she could do to keep from crumbling.

The coffee grew cold, the doughnuts stale. The bystanders watched with growing restlessness, no longer tapping their feet to the music but looking more somber with each passing minute. There were conferences—between Edgar, Anne, Marni and Web, between Dan, Edgar and Web, between Cynthia, Anne and Marni.

Nothing helped.

As a final resort, when they were well into the fourth hour of the shot, Web turned on a small fan to stir Marni's hair from behind. He showed her how to stand, showed her how to slowly sway her body and gently swing her arms, told her to lower her chin and look directly at him.

She followed his instructions to the letter, in truth so exhausted that she was dipping into a reserve of sheer grit. She couldn't take much more, she knew. She *wouldn't* take much more. Wasn't she the one in command here? Wasn't she the employer of every last person in the room?

While she ran the gamut of indignant thought, Web stood back and studied her, and for the first time in hours he felt he might have something special. Moving that way, with her hair billowing softly, she was the girl he remembered from that summer in Maine. She was direct and honest, serious but free, and she exuded the aura of power that came from success.

He caught his breath, then quickly raised his camera and prepared to shoot. "That's it, Oh, sunshine, that's it . . ."

Her movement stopped abruptly. *Sunshine*. It was what he'd always called her at the height of passion, when she would whisper that she loved him and would have to settle for an endearment in place of a returned vow.

It was the final straw. No longer able to stem the tears she'd fought so valiantly, she covered her face with her hands and, heedless of all around her, began to weep softly.

2

MARNI LANGE WAS on top of the world. Seventeen and eager to live life to its fullest, she'd just graduated from high school and would be entering Wellesley College in the fall. As they did every June, her parents, brother and sister and herself had come to their summer home in Camden, Maine, to sun and sail, barbecue and party to their hearts' content.

Ethan, her older brother by eight years, had looked forward to this particular summer as the first he'd be spending as a working man on vacation. Having graduated from business school, he'd spent the past eight months as a vice-president of the Lange Corporation, which had been formed by their father, Jonathan, some thirty years before. Privileged by being the son of the founder, president and chairman of the board of the corporation, Ethan was, like his father, conducting what work he had to do during the summer months from Camden.

Tanya, Marni's older sister by two years, had looked forward to the summer as a well-earned vacation from college, which she was attending only because her parents had insisted on it. If she'd had her way she'd be traveling the world, dallying with every good-looking man in sight. College men bored her nearly as much as her classes did, she'd discovered quickly. She needed an older man, she bluntly claimed, a man with experience and savvy and style.

Marni felt light-years away from her sister, and always had. They were as different as night and day in looks, personality and aspirations. While Tanya was intent on having a good time until the day she reeled in the oil baron who would free her from her parents and assure her of the good life forever, Marni was quieter, serious about commitment yet fun-loving. She wanted to get an education, then perhaps go out to work for a while, and the major requirement she had for a husband was that he adore her.

A husband was the last thing on her mind that summer, though. She was young. She'd dated aplenty, partying gaily within society's elite circles, but she'd never formed a relationship she would have called deep. Too many of the young men she'd known seemed shallow, unable to discuss world news or the stock market or the latest nonfiction best-seller. She wanted to grow, to meet interesting people, to broaden her existence before she thought of settling down.

The summer began as it always did, with reunion parties among the families whose sumptuous homes, closed all winter, were now buzzing with life. Marni enjoyed seeing friends she hadn't seen since the summer before, and she felt that much more buoyant with both her high school degree and her college acceptance letter lying on the desk in her room back at the Langes' Long Island estate.

After the reunions came the real fun—days of yachting along the Maine coast, hours sunning on the beach or hanging out on the town green or cruising the narrow roads in late-model cars whose almost obscene luxury was fully taken for granted by the young people in question.

Marni had her own group of friends, as did Tanya, but for very obvious reasons both groups tagged along with Ethan and his friends whenever possible. Ethan never put up much of a fight . . . for equally obvious reasons. Though his own tastes ran toward shapely brunettes a year or two

older than Tanya, he knew that several of his group pre-
ferred the even younger blood of Marni's friends.

It was because of the latter, or perhaps because Ethan was
feeling restless about something he couldn't understand,
that this particular summer he made a new friend. His last
name was Webster, but the world knew him simply as
Web—at least, the world that came into contact with the
Camden Inn and Resort where he was employed alter-
nately as lifeguard, bellboy and handyman.

Ethan had been using the pool when he struck up that first
conversation with Web, whom he discovered to be far more
interesting than any of the friends he was with. Web was
twenty-six, footloose and fancy-free, something which, for
all his social and material status, Ethan had never been.
While Ethan had jetted from high-class hotel to high-class
hotel abroad, Web had traveled the world on freighters,
passenger liners or any other vehicle on which he could find
employment. While Ethan, under his father's vigilant eye,
had met and hobnobbed with the luminaries of the world,
Web had read about them in the quiet of whatever small
room he was renting at the time.

Web was as educated as he and perhaps even brighter,
Ethan decided early on in their friendship, and the luxury
of Web's life was that he was beholden to no one. Ethan en-
vied and admired it to the extent that he found himself
spending more and more time with Web.

It was inevitable that Marni should meet him, nearly as
inevitable that she should be taken with him from the first.
He was mature. He was good-looking. He was carefree and
adventurous, yet soft-spoken and thoughtful. Given the
diverse and oftentimes risky things he'd experienced in life,
there was an excitement about him that Marni had never
found in another human being. He was free. He was his own
man.

He was also a roamer. She knew that well before she fell in love with him, but that didn't stop it from happening. Puppy love, Ethan had called it, infatuation. But Marni knew differently.

After her introduction to Web, she was forever on Ethan's tail. At first she tried to be subtle. She'd just come for a swim, she told Web minutes before she dived into the resort pool, leaving the two men behind to talk. But she wore her best bikini and made sure that the lounge chair she stretched out on in the sun was well within Web's range of vision.

She tagged along with Ethan when he and Web went out boating, claiming that she had nothing to do at home and was bored. She sandwiched herself into the back of Ethan's two-seater sports car when he and Web drove to Bar Harbor on Web's day off, professing that she needed a day off too from the monotony of Camden. She sat intently, with her chin in her palm, while the two played chess in Web's small room at the rear of the Inn, insisting that she'd never learn the game unless she could observe two masters at it.

Ethan and Web did other things, wilder things—racing the wind on the beach at two in the morning on the back of Web's motorcycle, playing pool and drinking themselves silly at a local tavern, diving by moonlight to steal lobsters from traps not far from shore, then boiling them in a pot over a fire on the sand. Marni wasn't allowed to join them at such times, but she knew where they went and what they did, and it added to her fascination for Web...as did the fact that Jonathan and Adele Lange thoroughly disapproved of him.

Marni had never been perverse or rebellious where her parents were concerned. She'd enjoyed her share of mischief when she'd been younger, and still took delight in the occasional scheme that drew arched brows and pursed lips from her parents. But Web drew far more than that.

"Who *is* he?" her mother would ask when Ethan announced that he was meeting with Web yet again. "Where does he come from?"

"Lots of places," Ethan would answer, indulging in his own adult prerogative for independence.

Jonathan Lange agreed wholeheartedly with his wife. "But you don't know anything about the man, Ethan. For all you know, he's been on the wrong side of the law at some point in his, uh, illustrious career."

"Maybe," Ethan would say with a grin. "But he happens to know a hell of a lot about a hell of a lot. He's an extension of my education . . . like night school. Look at it that way."

The elder Langes never did, and Web's existence continued to be viewed as something distasteful. He was never invited to the Lange home, and he became the scapegoat for any and all differences of opinion the Langes had with their son. Starry-eyed, Marni didn't believe a word her parents said in their attempts to discredit Web. If anything, their dislike of him added an element of danger, of challenge, to her own attempts to catch his eye.

She liked looking at him—at his deeply tanned face, which sported the bluest of eyes; his brown hair, which had been kissed golden by the sun; his knowing and experienced hands. His body was solid and muscular, and his fluid, lean-hipped walk spoke of self-assurance. She knew he liked looking at her, too, for she'd find him staring at her from time to time, those blue eyes alight with desire. At least she thought it was desire. She never really knew, because he didn't follow up on it. Oh, he touched her—held her hand to help her from the car, bodily lifted her from the boat to the dock, stopped in his rounds of the pool to add a smidgen of suntan lotion to a spot she'd missed on her back—but he never let his touch wander, as increasingly she wished he would.

Frustration became a mainstay in her existence. She dressed her prettiest when she knew she'd see Web, made sure her long auburn hair was clean and shiny, painted her toenails and fingernails in hopes of looking older. But, for whatever his reasons, Web kept his distance, and short of physically attacking the man, Marni didn't know what more she could do.

Then came a day when Ethan was ill. Web was off duty, and the two had planned to go mountain climbing, but Ethan had been sick to his stomach all night and could barely lift his head come morning. Marni, who'd spent the previous two days pestering Ethan to take her along, was sitting on his bed at seven o'clock.

"I'll go in your place," she announced, leaning conspiratorially close. Her parents were still in bed at the other end of the house.

"You will not," Ethan managed to say through dry lips. He closed his eyes and moaned. "God, do I feel awful."

"I'm going, Ethan. Web has been looking forward to this—I heard him talking. There's no reason in the world why he has to either cancel or go alone."

"For Pete's sake, Marni, don't be absurd."

"There's nothing absurd about my going mountain climbing."

"With Web there is. You'll slow him down."

"I won't. I've got more energy than you do even when you're well. I've got youth on my side."

"Exactly. And you think Web's going to *want* you along? You're seventeen and absolutely drooling for him. Come on, sweetheart. Be realistic. We both know why you want to go, and it's got nothing to do with the clean, fresh air." He rolled to his side, tucked his knees up and moaned again.

Marni knew he was indulgent when it came to her attraction for Web. He humored her, never quite taking her seriously. So, she mused, fair was fair . . . "Okay, then. I'll go over to his place and explain that you can't go."

"Call him."

She was already on her feet. "I'll go over. *He* can be the one to make the decision." And she left.

Web was more than surprised to find Marni on his doorstep at the very moment Ethan should have been. He was also slightly wary. "You're trying to trick me into something, Marni Lange," he accused, with only a half smile to take the edge off his voice.

"I'm not, Web. I like the outdoors, and I've climbed mountains before."

"When?" he shot back.

"When I was at camp."

"How long ago?"

"Four . . . five years."

"Ahhh. Those must have been quite some mountains you twelve-year-old girls climbed."

"They were mountains, no less than the one you and Ethan were planning to climb."

"Hmmph. . . . Do your parents know you're here?"

"What's that got to do with anything?"

"Do they know?"

"They know I won't be home till late." She paused, then at Web's arched brow added more sheepishly, "I told them I was driving with a couple of friends down to Old Orchard. They won't worry. I'm a big girl."

"That's right," he said, very slowly dropping his gaze along the lines of her body. It was the first time he'd looked at her that way, and Marni felt a ripple of excitement surge through her because there was a special spark that was never in his eyes when Ethan was around. It was the spark that kept her spirits up when he went on to drawl, "You're a big girl, all right. Seventeen years old."

When she would have argued—like the seventeen-year-old she was—she controlled herself. "My age doesn't have anything to do with my coming today or not," she said with what she hoped was quiet reserve. "I'd really like to go mountain climbing, and since you'd planned to do it anyway, I didn't see any harm in asking to join you. Ethan would have been here if he hadn't been sick." She turned and took a step away from his door. "Then again, maybe you'd rather wait till he's better."

She was halfway down the hall when he called her back, and she was careful to look properly subdued when he grabbed his things from just inside the door, shut it behind him, then collared her with his hand and propelled them both off.

It was the most beautiful day Marni had ever spent. Web drove her car—he smilingly claimed that he didn't trust her experience, or lack of it, at the wheel—and they reached the appointed mountain by ten. It wasn't a huge mountain, though it was indeed higher and steeper than any Marni had ever climbed. She held her own, though, taking Web's offered hand over tough spots for the sake of the delicious contact more than physical necessity.

The day had started out chilly but warmed as they went, and they slowly peeled off layers of clothing and stuffed them in their backpacks. By the time they stopped for lunch, Marni was grateful for the rest. She'd brought along the food Cook had packed for Ethan and had made one addition of her own—a bottle of wine pilfered quite remorselessly from the huge stock in the Langes' cellar.

"Nice touch," Web mused, skillfully uncorking the wine and pouring them each a paper cup full. "Maybe not too wise, though. A little of this and we're apt to have a tough time of it on the way back down."

"There's beer if you prefer," Marni pointed out gently. "Ethan had it already chilled, so evidently he wasn't worried about its effects."

"No, no. Wine's fine." He sipped it, then cocked his head. "It suits you. I can't imagine your drinking beer."

"Why not?"

He propped himself on an elbow and crossed his legs at the ankle. Then he looked at her, studying her intently. Finally, he reached for a thick ham sandwich. "You're more delicate than beer," he said, his eyes focusing nowhere in particular.

"If that's a compliment, I thank you," she said, making great efforts—and succeeding overall—to hide her glee. She helped herself to a sandwich and leaned back against a tree. "This is nice. Very quiet. Peaceful."

"You like peaceful places?"

"Not all the time," she mused softly, staring off into the woods. "I like activity, things happening, but this is the best kind of break." And the best kind of company, she might have added if she'd dared. She didn't dare.

"Are you looking forward to going to Wellesley?"

Her bright eyes found his. "Oh, yes. It was my first choice. I was deferred for early admission—I guess my board scores weren't as high as they might have been—and if I hadn't gotten in I suppose I would have gone somewhere else and been perfectly happy. But I'm glad it never came down to that."

Web asked her what she wanted to study, and she told him. He asked what schools her friends were going to, and she told him. He asked what she wanted to do with her future, and she told him—up to a point. She didn't say that she wanted a husband and kids and a house in Connecticut because she'd simply taken that all for granted, and it somehow seemed inappropriate to say to Web. He wasn't the house-in-Connecticut type. At this precise moment, being with him as she'd dreamed of being so often, she wasn't either.

They talked more as they ate. Web was curious about her life, and she eagerly answered his questions. She asked some of her own about the jobs he'd had and their accompanying adventures, and with minor coaxing he regaled her with tales, some tall, some not. They worked steadily through the bottle of wine, and by the time it was done and every bit of their lunch had been demolished, they were both feeling rather lazy.

"See? What did I tell you?" Web teased. He lay on his back with his head pillowed on his arms. Marni was in a similar position not far from him. He tipped his head and warmed her with his blue eyes. "We might never get down from this place."

Her heart was fluttering. "We haven't reached the top yet."

"We will. It's just a little way more, and the trip down is faster and easier. Only thing is—" he paused to bend one knee up "—I'm not sure I want to move."

"There's no rush," she said softly.

"No," he mused thoughtfully. His eyes held hers for a long time before he spoke in a deep, very quiet, subtly warning voice. "Don't look at me that way, Marni."

"What way?" she breathed.

"*That* way. I'm only human."

She didn't know if he was pleased or angry. "I'm sorry. I didn't mean—"

"Of course you didn't mean. You're seventeen. How are you supposed to know what happens when you look at a man that way?"

"What way?"

"With your heart on your sleeve."

"Oh." She looked away. She hadn't realized she'd been so transparent, and she was sure she'd made Web uncomfortable. "I'm sorry," she murmured.

Neither of them said anything for a minute, and Marni stared blindly at a nearby bush.

"Ah, hell," Web growled suddenly, and grabbed her arm. "Come over here. I want you smiling, not all misty-eyed."

"I wasn't misty-eyed," she argued, but she made no argument when he pulled her head to the crook of his shoulder. "It's just that...maybe Ethan was right. I am a pest. You didn't want me along today. I'm only seventeen."

"You were the one who pointed out that your age was irrelevant to your going mountain climbing."

"It is. But . . ." Her cheeks grew red, and she couldn't finish. It seemed she was only making things worse.

He brushed a lock of hair from her hot cheek and tucked it behind her ear. The action brought his forearm close to her face. Marni closed her eyes, breathed in the warm male scent of his skin, knew she was halfway to heaven and was about to be tossed back down.

"I think it's about time we talk about this, Marni," he said, continuing to gently stroke her hair. "You're seventeen and I'm twenty-six. We have a definite problem here."

"I'm the one with the problem," she began, but Web was suddenly on his elbow leaning over her.

"Is that what you think . . . that you're the only one?"

Her gaze was unsteady, faintly hopeful. "Am I wrong?"

"Very."

She held her breath.

"You're a beautiful woman," he murmured as his eyes moved from one of her features to the next.

"I'm a girl," she whispered.

"That's what I keep trying to tell myself, but my body doesn't seem to want to believe it. I've tried, Marni. For the past month I've tried to keep my hands off. It was dangerous to come here today."

Marni reached heaven by leaps and bounds. Her body began to relax against his, and she grew aware of his firm lines, his strength. "You didn't do it single-handedly."

"But I'm older. I should know better."

"Are there rules that come with age?"

"There's common sense. And my common sense tells me that I shouldn't be lying here with you curled against me this way."

"You were the one who pulled me over," she pointed out.

"And you're not protesting."

She couldn't possibly protest when she was floating on a cloud of bliss. "Would you like me to?"

"Damn right I would. One of us should show some measure of sanity."

"There's nothing insane about this," she murmured, distracted because she'd let her hand glide over his chest. She could feel every muscle, every crinkling hair beneath his T-shirt, even the small dot of his nipple beneath her palm.

"No?" he asked. Abruptly he flipped over and was on top of her. His blue eyes grilled hers heatedly, and his voice was hoarse. "Y'know, Marni, I'm not one of your little high school friends, or even one of the college guys I'm sure you've dated." He took both of her hands and anchored them by her shoulders. Though his forearms took some of his weight, the boldness of his body imprinted itself on hers. "I've had women. Lots of them. If one of them were here instead of you, we wouldn't be playing around. We'd be stark naked and we'd be making love already."

Marni didn't know where she found the strength to speak. His words—the experience and maturity and adventure they embodied—set her on fire. Her blood was boiling, and her bones were melting. "Is that what we're doing... playing?"

He shifted his lower body in apt answer to her question, then arched a brow at the flare of color in her cheeks. "You don't want to play, do you? You want it all."

She was breathing faster. "I just want you to kiss me," she managed to whisper. The blatancy of his masculinity was reducing her to mush.

"Just a kiss?" he murmured throatily. "Okay, Marni Lange, let's see how you kiss."

She held her breath as he lowered his head, then felt the touch of his mouth on hers for the first time. His lips were hot, and she drew back, scalded, only to find that his heat was tempting, incendiary where the rest of her body was concerned. So she didn't pull back when he touched her a second time, and her lips quickly parted beneath the urging of his.

He tasted and caressed, then drank with unslaked thirst. Marni responded on instinct, kissing him back, feeding on his hunger, willingly offering the inside of her mouth and her tongue when he sought them out.

His breathing was as unsteady as hers when he drew back and looked at her again. "You don't kiss like a seventeen-year-old."

She gave a timid smile. She'd never before received or responded to a kiss like that, but she didn't want Web to know how inexperienced she really was. "I run in fast circles."

"Is that so?" His mouth devoured her smile in a second mind-bending kiss, and he released one of her hands and framed her throat, slowly drawing his palm down until the fullness of her breast throbbed beneath it. "God, Marni, you're lovely," he rasped. "Lovely and strong and fresh . . ."

Her hands were in his hair, sifting through its thickness as she held him close. "Kiss me again," she pleaded.

"I may be damned for this," he murmured under his breath, "but I want it, too." So he kissed her many, many more times, and he touched her breasts and her belly and her thighs. When his hand closed over the spot where he wanted most to be, she arched convulsively.

"Tell me, Marni," he panted next to her ear, "I need to know. Have you done this before?"

She knew he'd stop if she told him the truth, and one part of her ached so badly she was tempted to lie. But she wasn't irresponsible. Nor could she play the role of the conniving female. He'd know, one way or the other. "No," she finally whispered, but with obvious regret.

Web held himself still, suspended above her for a moment, then gave a loud groan and rolled away.

She was up on her elbow in an instant. "Web? It doesn't matter. I want to. Most of my friends—"

"I don't give a damn about most of your friends," he growled, throwing an arm over his eyes. "You're seventeen, the kid sister of a man who's become my good friend. I can't do it."

"Don't you want to?"

He lifted his arm and stared at her, then grabbed her hand and drew it down to cover the faded fly of his jeans. The fabric was strained. He pressed her hand against his fullness, then groaned again and rolled abruptly to his side away from her.

Her question had been answered quite eloquently. Marni felt the knot of frustration in her belly, but she'd also felt his. "Can I . . . can I do something?" she whispered, wanting to satisfy him almost as much as she wanted to be satisfied herself.

"Oh, you can do something," was his muffled reply, "but it'd only shock you and I don't think you're ready for that."

She leaned over him. "I'm ready, Web. I want to do it."

Glaring, he rolled back to face her, but his glare faded when he saw the sincerity of her expression. His eyes grew soft, his features compassionate. He raised a hand to gently stroke the side of her face. "If you really want to do something," he murmured, "you can help me clean up here, then race me to the top of this hill and down. By the time we're back at the bottom, we should both be in control. Either that," he added with a wry smile, "or too tired to do anything about it."

It was his smile and the ensuing swelling of her heart that first told Marni she was in love. Over the next week she pined, because Web made sure that they weren't alone again. He looked at her though, and she could see that he wasn't immune to her. He went out of his way not to touch her and, much as she craved those knowing hands on her again, she didn't push him for fear she'd come across as being exactly what she was—a seventeen-year-old girl with hots that were nearly out of control. She knew that in time she could get through to Web. He felt something for her, something strong. But time was her enemy. The summer was half over, and though she wanted it to last forever, it wouldn't.

She was right on the button when it came to Web and his feelings for her. He wasn't immune, not by a long shot. He told himself it was crazy, that he'd never before craved untried flesh, but there was something more that attracted him to her, something that the women he'd had, the women he continued to have, didn't possess.

So when a group of Ethan's friends and their dates gathered for a party at someone's boat house, Web quite helplessly dragged Marni to a hidden spot and kissed her willing lips until they were swollen.

"What was that for?" she asked. Her arms were around his neck, and she was on tiptoe, her back pressed to the weathered board of the house.

"Are you protesting?" he teased, knowing she'd returned the kiss with a fever.

"No way. Just curious. You've gone out of your way to avoid me." She didn't quite pout, but her accusation was clear.

He insinuated his body more snugly against hers. "I've tried. Again . . . still. It's not working." He framed her face with his hands, burying his fingers in her hair. "I want you, Marni. I lie in bed at night remembering that day on the mountain and how good you felt under me, and I tell myself that it's nonsense, but the chemistry's there, damn it."

"I know," she agreed in an awed whisper.

"So what are we going to do about it?"

She shrugged, then drew her hands from his shoulders to lightly caress the strong cords of his neck. "You can make love to me if you want."

"Is it what you want?" His soberness compelled her to meet his gaze.

She blinked, her only show of timidity. "I've wanted it for days now. I feel so . . . empty when I think of you. I get this ache . . . way down low . . ."

"Your parents would kill you. And me."

"There are different kinds of killing. Right now I'm dying because I want you, and I'm afraid you still think of me as a little kid who's playing with fire. I may only be seventeen, but I've been with enough men to know when I find one who's different."

He could have substituted his own age for hers and repeated the statement. He didn't understand it, but it was the truth, and it went beyond raw chemistry. Marni had a kind of depth he'd never found in a woman before. He'd watched her participate in conversations with Ethan and his friends, holding her own both intellectually and emotionally. She was sophisticated beyond her years, perhaps not physically, but he felt that urgency in her now.

"I'm serious about your parents," he finally said. "They dislike me as it is. If I up and seduce their little girl—"

"You're not seducing me. It's a mutual thing." Made bold by the emotions she felt when she was in this man's arms, she slid her hand between their bodies and gently caressed the hard evidence of his sex. "I've never done this to another man, never touched another man this way," she whispered. "And I'm not afraid, because when I do this to you—" she rotated her palm and felt him shudder and arch into it "—I feel it inside me, too. Please, Web. Make love to me."

Her nearness, the untutored but instinctively perfect motion of her hand, was making it hard for him to breathe. "Can you get out later?" he managed in a choked whisper.

"Tonight? I think so."

He set her back, leaving his fingers digging into her shoulders. "Think about it until then, and if you still feel the same way, come to me. I'll be on the beach behind the Wayward Pines at two o'clock. You know the one."

She nodded, unable to say a word as the weight of what she was about to agree to settled on her shoulders. He left her then to return to the group. She went straight home and sat in the darkness of her room, giving herself every reason why she should undress and go to sleep for the night but knowing that she'd never sleep, that her body tingled all over, that her craving was becoming obsessive, and that she loved Web.

It didn't seem to matter that he was a roamer, that he'd be gone at the end of the summer, that he couldn't offer her any kind of future. The fact was that she loved him and that she wanted him to be the first man to know, to teach her the secrets of her body.

Wearing nothing but a T-shirt, cutoffs and sandals, she stole out of the house at one-forty-five and ran all the way to the beach. It was an isolated strip just beyond an aging house whose owner visited rarely. As its name suggested, tall pines loomed uncharacteristically close to the shore, giving it a sheltered feeling, a precious one.

Web was propped against the tallest of the pines, and her heart began to thud when he straightened. Out of breath, and now breathless for other reasons, she stopped, then advanced more slowly.

"I wasn't sure you'd come," he said softly, his eyes never leaving hers as he held out his hand.

"I had to," was all she said, ignoring his hand and throwing her arms around his neck. His own circled her, lifting her clear off her feet, and he held her tightly as he buried his face in her hair.

Then he set her down and loosened his grip. "Are you sure? Are you sure this is what you want?"

In answer, she reached for the hem of her T-shirt and drew it over her head. She hadn't worn a bra. Her pert breasts gleamed in the pale moonlight. Less confidently, she reached for one of his hands and put it on her swelling flesh. "Please, Web. Touch me. Teach me."

He didn't need any further encouragement. He dipped his head and took her lips while his hands explored the curves of her breasts, palms kneading in circles, fingers moving inexorably toward the tight nubs that puckered for him.

She cried out at the sweet torment he created, and reached for him, needing to touch him, to know him as he was coming to know her. He held her off only long enough for him to whip his own T-shirt over his head, then he hauled her against him and embraced her with arms that trembled.

"Oh, Web!" she gasped when their flesh came together.

"Feels nice, doesn't it?" His voice held no smugness, only the same awe hers had held. She was running her hands over his back, pressing small kisses to his throat. "Easy, Marni," he whispered hoarsely. "Let's just take it slow this first time."

"I don't think I can," she cried. "I feel . . . I feel . . ."

He smiled. His own hands had already covered her back and were dipping into the meager space at the back of her shorts. "I know." He dragged in a shuddering breath, then said more thickly, "Let's get these off." He was on his knees then, unsnapping and unzipping her shorts, tugging them down. She hadn't worn panties. He sucked in his breath. "Marni!"

Her legs were visibly shaking, and she was clutching his sinewed shoulders for support. "Please don't think I'm awful, Web. I just want you so badly!"

He pressed his face to her naked stomach, then spread kisses even lower. "Not any more so than I want you," he whispered. Then he was on his feet, tugging at the snaps of his jeans, pushing the denim and his briefs down and off.

Seconds later they were tumbling onto the sand, their greedy bodies straining to feel more of the other's, hands equally as rapacious. Marni was inflamed by his size, his strength, the manly scent that mixed with that of the pines and the salty sea air to make her drunk. She felt more open than she'd ever been in her life, but more protected.

And more loved. Web didn't say the words, but his hands gave her a message as they touched her. They were hungry and restless, but ever gentle as they stimulated her, leaving no inch of her body untouched. Her breasts, her back, her belly, thighs and bottom—nothing escaped him, nor did she want it to. If she'd ever thought she'd feel shy at exposing herself this way to a man, the desire, the love she felt ruled that out. There was a rightness to Web's liberty, a rightness to the feel of his lips on her body, to the feel of his weight settling between her thighs.

Her fingers dug into the lean flesh of his hips, urging him down, crying wordlessly for him to make her his. She felt his fingers between her legs, and she arched against him as he stroked her.

"Marni . . . Marni," he whispered as one finger ventured even deeper. "Oh, sunshine, you're so ready for me . . . how did I ever deserve this . . ."

"Please . . . now . . . I need you . . ." When he pulled back, she whimpered, "Web?"

"It's okay." He was reaching behind him. "I need to protect you." He took a small foil packet from the pocket of his jeans and within minutes was back, looming over her, finding that hot, enfolding place between her splayed thighs.

He poised himself, then stroked her cheeks with his thumbs. "Kiss me, sunshine," he commanded deeply.

She did, and she felt him begin to enter her. It was the most wonderful, most frustrating experience yet. She thrust her hips upward, not quite realizing that it was her own inner body that resisted him.

He was breathing heavily, his lips against hers. "Sweet...so sweet. A bit of pain...a blaze of glory..." Then he surged forward, forcefully rupturing the membrane that gave proof of her virginity but was no more.

She cried out at the sharp pain, but it eased almost immediately.

"Okay?" he asked, panting as she was, holding himself still inside her while her torn flesh accommodated itself to him. It was all he could do not to climax there and then. She was so tight, so sleek, so hot and new and all his.

"Okay," she whispered tightly.

"Just relax," he crooned. He ducked his head and teased the tip of her nipple with his tongue. "I'm inside you now," he breathed, warm against that knotted bud. "Let's go for the glory."

She couldn't say a word then, for he withdrew partway, gently returned, withdrew a little more, returned with growing ardor, withdrew nearly completely, returned with a slam, and the feel of him inside her, stroking that dark, hidden part was so astonishing, so electric that she could only clutch his shoulders and hang on.

Nothing else mattered at that moment but Web. Marni wasn't thinking of her parents and how furious they'd be, of her brother and how shocked he'd be, of her friends and how envious they'd be. She wasn't thinking of the past or the future, simply the present.

"I love you," she cried over and over again. His presence had become part and parcel of her being. Without fear, she raised her hips to his rhythm, and rather than discomfort she felt an excitement that grew and grew until she was sure she'd simply explode.

"Ahhh, sunshine . . . so good . . . that's it . . . oh, God!"

His body was slick above hers, their flesh slapping together in time with the waves on the shore. Then that sound too fell aside, and all awareness was suspended as first Marni, then Web, strained and cried out, one body, then the next, breaking into fierce orgasmic shudders.

It was a long time before either of them spoke, a long time before the spasms slowed and their gasps quieted to a more controlled breathing. Web slid to her side and drew her tightly into his arms. "You are something, Marni Lange," he whispered against her damp forehead.

"Web . . . Web . . . unbelievable!"

He gave a deep, satisfied, purely male laugh. "I think I'd have to agree with you."

She nestled her head more snugly against his breast. "Then I . . . I did okay?"

"You did more than okay. You did *super*."

She smiled. "Thank you." She raised her head so that she could see those blue, blue eyes she adored. At night, in the moonlight, they were a beacon. "Thank you, Web," she said more softly. "I wanted you to be the first. It was very special . . . very, very special." She wanted to say again that she loved him, but he hadn't returned the words, and she didn't want to put him on the spot. She was grateful for what she felt, for what he'd made her feel, for what he'd given her. For the time being it was more than enough.

They rested in each other's arms for a while, listening to the sounds of the sea until those became too tempting to resist. So they raced into the water, laughing, playing, finally making love again there in the waves, wrapped up enough in each other not to care whether the rest of the world saw or heard or knew.

In the two weeks that followed, they were slightly more cautious. Unable to stay away from each other, they timed their rendezvous with care, meeting at odd hours and in odd places where they could forget the rest of the world existed and could live those brief times solely for each other and themselves. Marni was wildly happy and passionately in love; that justified her actions. She found Web to be intelligent and worldly, exquisitely sensitive and tender when she was in his arms. Web only knew that there was something special about her, something bright and luminous.

She was a free spirit, forthright and fresh. She was a ray of sunshine in his life.

Marni's parents suspected that something was going on, but Marni always had a ready excuse to give them when they asked where she was going or where she'd been, and she was careful never to mention Web's name. Ethan knew what was happening and, though he worried, he adored Marni and was fond enough of Web to trust that he was in control of things. Tanya was jealous, plainly and simply. She'd been stringing along another of Ethan's friends for most of the summer, but when—inevitably, through one of Marni's friends—she got wind of Marni's involvement with Web, she suddenly realized what she'd overlooked and sought to remedy the situation. Web wasn't interested, which only irked her all the more, and at the time Marni made no attempt to reason with her sister.

It was short-sighted on her part, but then none of them ever dreamed that the summer would end prematurely and tragically.

With a week left before Labor Day, Web and Ethan set out in search of an evening's adventure in the university town of Orono. Marni had wanted to come along, but Ethan had been adamant. He claimed that their parents had been questioning him about her relationship with Web, and that the best way to mollify them would be for him to take off with Web while she spent the evening home for a change. She'd still protested, whereupon Ethan had conned Web into taking the motorcycle. It only sat two; there was no room for her.

For months and months after that, Marni would go over the what ifs again and again. What if she hadn't pestered and the two had taken Ethan's car as they'd originally planned? What if she'd made noise enough to make them cancel the trip? What if her parents hadn't been suspicious of her relationship with Web? What if there hadn't been anything to be suspicious of? But all the what ifs in the world—and there were even more she grappled with—couldn't change the facts.

It had begun to rain shortly after eleven. The road had been dark. Two cars had collided at a blind intersection. The motorcycle had skidded wildly in their wake. Ethan had been thrown, had hit a tree and had been killed instantly.

3

"OKAY," WEB SIGHED, straightening. "That's it for today."

Anne rushed to him, her eyes on Marni's hunched form. "But you haven't got what you want," she argued in quiet concern.

"I know that and you know that, but Marni's in no shape to give us anything else right now." He handed his camera to an assistant, then raked a hand through his hair. "I'm not sure I am either," he said. In truth he was disgusted with himself. Sunshine. How could he have slipped that way? He hadn't planned to do it; the endearment had just come out. But then, it appeared he'd handled Marni wrong from the start.

Dismayed murmurs filtered through the room, but Web ignored them to approach the stool where Marni sat. He put an arm around her shoulder and bent his head close, using his body as a shield between her and any onlookers. "I'm sorry, Marni. That was my fault. It wasn't intentional, believe me."

She was crying silently, whitened fingers pressed to her downcast face.

"Why don't you go on in and change. We'll make a stab at this another day."

She shook her head, but said nothing. Web crooked his finger at Anne, then, when she neared, tossed his head in the direction of the dressing room and left the two women alone.

"Come on, Marni," Anne said softly. It was her arm around Marni's shoulders now, and she was gently urging her to her feet.

"I've spoiled everything," Marni whispered, "and made a fool of myself in the process."

"You certainly have not," Anne insisted as they started slowly toward the dressing room. "We all knew you weren't wild about doing this. So you've shown us that you're human, and that there are some kinds of pressure you just can't take."

"We'll have to get someone else for the cover."

"Let's talk about that when you've calmed down."

Anne stayed with her while she changed into her own clothes. She was blotting at the moistness below her eyes when a knock came at the door. Anne answered it, then stepped outside, and Web came in, closing the door behind him.

"Are you okay?" he asked, leaning against the door. Though he barred her escape, he made no move to come closer.

She nodded.

"Maybe you were right," he said. "Maybe there are too many people around. You felt awkward. I should have insisted they leave."

She stared at him for a minute. "That was only part of the problem."

He returned her stare with one of his own. "I know."

"I told you I couldn't do this."

"We'll give it another try."

"No. I'm not going through it again."

He blinked. "It'll be easier next time. Fewer people. And I'll know what not to do."

Marni shook her head. "I'm not going through it again."

"Because it brought back memories?"

"Exactly."

"Memories you don't want."

"Memories that bring pain."

"But if you don't face them, they'll haunt you forever."

"They haven't haunted me before today."

He didn't believe her. She probably didn't dwell on those memories any more than he did, but he knew there were moments, fleeting moments when memory clawed at his gut. He couldn't believe she was callous enough not to have similar experiences. "Maybe you've repressed them."

"Maybe so. But I can't change the past."

"Neither can I. But there are still things that gnaw at me from time to time."

Marni held up a hand. "I don't want to get into this. I can't. Not now. Besides, I have to get into the office. I've already wasted enough time on this fiasco."

Web took a step closer. His voice was calm, too calm, his expression hard. "This is what I do for a living, Marni. I'm successful at it, and I'm respected. Don't you ever, ever call it a fiasco."

Too late she realized that she'd hit a sore spot. Her voice softened. "I'm sorry. I didn't mean it that way. I respect what you are and what you do, too, or else we'd never be paying you the kind of money we are. The fiasco was in using me for a model, particularly given what you and I had...what we had once." She looked away to find her purse, then, head bent, moved toward the door.

"I'm taking you to dinner tonight," Web announced quietly.

Her head shot up. "Oh, no. That would be rubbing salt in the wound."

"Maybe it would be cleansing it, getting the infection out. It's been festering, Marni. For fourteen years it's been festering. Maybe neither of us was aware of it. Maybe we never would have been if we hadn't run into each other today. But it's there, and I don't know about you, but I won't be able to put it out of my mind until we've talked. If we're going to work together—"

"We're not! That's what I keep trying to tell you! We tried today and failed, so it's done. Over. We'll get another model for the cover, and I can go back to what I do best."

"Burying your head in the sand?"

"I do *not* bury my head in the sand." Her eyes were flashing, but his were no less so, and the set of his jaw spoke of freshly stirred emotion.

"No? Fourteen years ago you said you loved me. Then I lay there after the accident, and you didn't visit me once, not once, Marni!" His teeth were gritted. "Two months I was in that hospital. *Two months*, and not a call, not a card, nothing."

Marni felt her eyes well anew with tears. "I can't talk about this," she whispered. "I can't handle it now."

"Tonight then."

She passed him and reached for the door, but he pressed a firm hand against it. "Please," she begged. "I have to go."

"Eight-thirty tonight. I'll pick you up at your place."

"No."

"I'll be there, Marni." He let his hand drop, and she opened the door. "Eight-thirty."

She shook her head, but said nothing more as she made good her escape. Unfortunately, Edgar and Steve, Anne, Cynthia, Dan and Marjorie were waiting for her. When they all started talking at once, she held up a hand.

"I'm going to the office." She looked at the crew from *Class*. "Go through your files, put your heads together and come up with several other suggestions for a cover face. Not necessarily a model, maybe someone in the business world. We'll meet about it tomorrow morning." She turned her attention to Edgar and Steve, but she was already moving away. "I'm taking the limousine. Are you coming?"

Without argument, they both hurried after her.

Web watched them go, a small smile on his lips. She could command when she wanted to, he mused, and she was quite a sight to behold. Five feet five inches of auburn-haired beauty, all fired up and decisive. She'd change her mind, of course, at least about doing the cover shot. He'd *make* her change her mind . . . if for no other reason than to prove to himself that, at last, he had what it took.

EIGHT-THIRTY THAT NIGHT found Marni sitting stiffly in her living room, her hands clenched in her lap. She jumped when the phone rang, wondering if Web had changed his mind. But it was the security guard calling from downstairs to announce that Brian Webster had indeed arrived.

She'd debated how to handle him and had known somehow that the proper way would *not* be to refuse to see him. She had more dignity than that, and more respect for Web professionally. Besides, he'd thrown an accusation at her earlier that day, and she simply had to answer it.

With a deep breath, she instructed the guard to send him up.

By the time the doorbell rang, her palms were damp. She rubbed them together, then blotted them on her skirt. It was the same skirt she'd worn that morning, the same jacket, the same blouse. She wanted Web to know that this was nothing more than an extension of her business day. Perhaps she wanted to remind herself of it. The prospect of having dinner with him was a little less painful that way.

What she hadn't expected was to open the door and find him wearing a stylish navy topcoat, between whose open lapels his dark suit, crisp white shirt and tie were clearly visible. He looked every bit as businesslike as she wanted to feel, but he threw her off-balance.

"May I come in?" he asked when she'd been unable to find her tongue.

"Uh, yes." She stood back dumbly. "Please do." She closed the door behind him.

"You seem surprised." Amused, he glanced down at himself. "Am I that shocking?"

"I, uh, I just didn't expect . . . I've never seen you in . . ."

"You didn't expect me to show up in a T-shirt and jeans, did you?"

"No, I . . . it's just . . ."

"Fourteen years, Marni. We all grow up at one point or another."

She didn't want to *touch* that one. "Can I . . . can I take your coat? Would you like a drink?" She hadn't planned to offer him any such thing, but then she didn't know quite *what* she'd planned. She couldn't just launch into an argument, not with him looking so . . . so urbane.

He shrugged out of the topcoat and set it on a nearby chair. "That would be nice. Bourbon and water, if you've got it," he said quietly, then watched her approach the bar at the far end of the room. She was still a little shaky, but he'd expected that. Hell, he was shaky, too, though he tried his best to hide it. "This is a beautiful place you've got." He admired the white French provincial decor, the original artwork on the walls. Everything was spotless and bright. "Have you been here long?"

"Three years," she said without turning. She was trying to pour the bourbon without splashing it all over the place. Her hands weren't terribly steady.

"Where were you before that?" he asked conversationally.

"I had another place. It was smaller. When I took over from . . . took over the presidency of the corporation, I realized I'd need a larger place for entertaining."

"Do you do much?"

She returned with his drink, her full concentration on keeping the glass steady. "Much?"

"Entertaining." He accepted the drink and sat back.

"Enough."

"Do you enjoy it?"

She took a seat across from him, half wishing she'd fixed a hefty something for herself but loathe to trust her legs a second time. "Sometimes."

He eyed her over the rim of his glass. "You must be very skilled at it . . . upbringing and all." He took a drink.

"I suppose you could say that. My family's always done its share of entertaining."

He nodded, threw his arm over the back of the sofa and looked around the room again. It was a diversionary measure. He wasn't quite sure what to say. Marni was uncomfortable. He wanted her to relax, but he wasn't sure how to achieve that. In the end, he realized that his best shot was with the truth.

"I wasn't sure you'd be here tonight. I was half worried that you'd find something else to do—a late meeting or a business dinner or a date."

She looked at her hands, tautly entwined in her lap, and spoke softly, honestly. "I haven't been good for much today, business or otherwise."

"But you went back to the office after you left the studio."

"For all the good it did me." She hadn't accomplished a thing, at least nothing that wouldn't have to be reexamined tomorrow. She'd been thoroughly distracted. She'd read contracts, talked on the phone, sat through a meeting, but for the life of her she couldn't remember what any of it had been about. She raised her eyes quickly, unable to hide the urgency she felt. "I want you to know something, Web. That time you were in the hospital . . . it wasn't that I wasn't thinking about you. I just . . . couldn't get away. I called the hospital to find out how you were, but I . . . I couldn't get there." Her eyes were growing misty again. It was the last thing Web wanted.

"I didn't come here to talk about that, Marni. I'm sorry I exploded that way this morning—"

"But you meant it. You're still angry—"

"Not this minute. And I really *didn't* come here to talk about it."

"You said we had to talk things out."

"We will. In time."

In time? In *future time?* "But we haven't got any time." She looked away, and her voice dropped. "We never really did. It seemed to run out barely before it had begun."

"We've got time. I spoke with Anne this afternoon. She agrees with me that you're still the best one for this cover. You said yourself that we're well ahead of the production schedule."

A spurt of anger brought Marni's gaze back to his. "I told you, it's done. I will not pose for that cover. You and Anne can conspire all you want, but I'm still the publisher of this magazine, and as such I have the final say. I'm not a child anymore, Web. I'm thirty-one now, not seventeen."

He sat forward and spoke gently. "I know that, Marni."

"I won't be told what's good for me and what isn't."

"Seems to me you could *never* be told that. In your own quiet way, you were headstrong even back then."

She caught her breath and bowed her head. "Not really."

"I don't believe you," was his quiet rejoinder. When she simply shrugged, he realized that she wasn't ready to go into that. In many respects, he wasn't either. He took another drink, then turned the glass slowly in his hands. "Look, Marni. I don't think either of us wants to rehash the past just yet. What I'd like—the real reason I'm here now—is for us to get to know each other. We've both changed in fourteen years. In addition to other things, we were friends once upon a time. I don't know about you, but I'm curious to know what my friend's been doing, what her life is like now."

"To what end?" There was a thread of desperation in her voice.

"To make it easier for us to shoot this picture, for one thing." When she opened her mouth to protest, he held up a hand and spoke more quickly. "I know. You're not doing it. But the reason you're not is that working with me stirs up a storm of memories. If we can get to know each other as adults—"

"You were an adult fourteen years ago. I was a child—"

"I was a man and you were a woman," he corrected, "but we were both pretty immature about some things."

She couldn't believe what he was saying. "You weren't immature," she argued. "You were experienced and worldly. You'd lived far more than I ever had."

"There's living, and there's living. But that's not the point. The point is that we've both changed. We've grown up. If we spend a little time together now, we can replace those memories with new ones. . . ." He stopped talking when he saw that she'd shrunk back into her seat. Was that dread in her eyes? He didn't want it to be. God, he didn't want that! He sat forward pleadingly. "Don't you see, Marni? You were shocked seeing me today because the last thing we shared involved pain for both of us. Sure, fourteen years have passed, but we haven't seen or spoken with each other in all that time. It's only natural that seeing each other would bring back all those other things. But it doesn't have to be like that. Not if we put something between those memories and us."

"I'm not sure I know what you're suggesting," she said in a tone that suggested she did.

"All I want," he went on with a sigh, "is to put the past aside for the time being. Hell, maybe it's a matter of pride for me. Maybe I want to show you what I've become. Is that so bad? Fourteen years ago, I was nothing. I wandered, I played. I never had more than a hundred bucks to my name at a given time. You had so much, at least in my eyes, and I'm not talking money now. You had a fine home, a family and social status."

Marni listened to his words, but it was his tone and his expression that reached her. He was sincere, almost beseechful. There was pain in his eyes, and an intense need. He'd never been quite that way with her fourteen years before, but she suddenly couldn't seem to separate the feelings she'd had for him then from the ache in her heart now. It occurred to her that the ache had begun when she'd first set eyes on him that morning. She'd attributed it to the pain of memory, and it was probably ninety-nine percent that, but there was something more, and she couldn't ignore it. Fourteen years ago she'd loved him. She didn't love him now, but there was still that...feeling. And those blue, blue eyes shimmering into her, captivating her, magnetizing her.

"I want to show you my world, Marni. I'm proud of it, and I want you to be proud, too. You may have thought differently, but my life was deeply affected by that summer in Camden." For a minute the blue eyes grew moist, but they cleared so quickly that Marni wondered if she'd imagined it. "Give me a chance, Marni. We'll start with dinner tonight. I won't pressure you for anything. I never did, did I?"

She didn't have to ponder that one. If anyone had done the pressuring—at least on the sexual level—it had been her. "No," she answered softly.

"And I won't do it now. You have my word on it. You also have my word that if anything gets too tough for you, I'll bring you back here and leave you alone. You *also* have my word that if, in the end, you decide you really can't do that cover, I'll abide by your decision. Fair?"

Fair? He was being so reasonable that she couldn't possibly argue. What wasn't fair was that he wore his suit so well, that his hair looked so thick and vibrant, that his features had matured with such dignity. But that wasn't his fault. Beauty was in the eye of the beholder.

She gave a rueful half smile and slowly nodded. "Fair."

He held her gaze a moment longer, as though he almost couldn't believe that she'd agreed, but his inner relief was such that he suddenly felt a hundred pounds lighter. He pushed back his cuff and glanced at the thin gold watch on his wrist.

"We've got reservations for five minutes ago. If I can use your phone, I'll let the maître d' know we're on our way."

She nodded and glanced toward the kitchen. When he rose and headed that way, she moved toward the small half bath off the living room. She suddenly wished she'd showered, done over her hair and makeup and changed into something fresher. Web was so obviously newly showered and shaved. She should have done more. But it was too late for that now, so the best she could do was to powder the faint shine from her nose and forehead, add a smidgen more blusher to her cheeks and touch up her lipstick.

Web was waiting when she emerged. He'd already put on his topcoat and was holding the coat she'd left ready and waiting nearby. It, too, was the same she'd worn that morning, but that decision she didn't regret. To wear silver fox with Web, even in spite of his own debonair appearance, seemed a little heavy-handed.

He helped her on with the coat, waited while she got her purse, then lightly took her elbow and escorted her to the door. They rode the elevator in a silence that was broken at last by Marni's self-conscious laugh. "You're very tall. I never wore high heels in Camden, but they don't seem to make a difference." She darted him a shy glance, but quickly returned her gaze to the patterned carpet.

He felt vaguely self-conscious, too. "I never wore shoes with laces in Camden. They add a little."

She nodded and said nothing more. The elevator door purred open. Web guided her through the plush lobby, then the enclosed foyer and finally to the street. He discreetly pressed a bill into the doorman's hand in exchange for the keys to his car, then showed Marni to the small black BMW parked at the curb. Before she could reach for it, he opened the door. "Buckle up," was all he said before he locked her in and circled the car to the driver's side.

The restaurant he'd chosen was a quiet but elegant one. The maître d' seemed not in the least piqued by their tardiness, greeting Web with a warm handshake and offering a similarly warm welcome to Marni when Web introduced them, before showing them to their table.

Web deftly ordered a wine. Then, when Marni had decided what she wanted to eat, he gave both her choice and his own to the waiter. Watching him handle himself, she decided he was as smooth in this urban setting as he'd been by the sea. He had always exuded a kind of confidence, and she assumed it would extend to whatever activity he was involved in. But seeing him here, comfortable in a milieu that should have been hers more than his, took some getting used to. It forced her to see him in a different light. She struggled to do that.

"Have you been here before?" he asked softly.

"For a business dinner once or twice. The food's excellent, don't you think?"

"I'm counting on it," he said with a grin. "So . . . tell me about Marni Lange and the Lange Corporation."

She shook her head. Somewhere along the line, she realized he was right. They'd been . . . friends once, and she *was* curious as to what he'd done in the past years. "You first. Tell me about Brian Webster the photographer."

"What would you like to know?"

"How you got started. I never knew you had an interest in photography."

"I didn't. At least, not when I knew you. But the year after that was a difficult one for me." His brow furrowed. "I took a good look at myself and didn't like what I saw."

She found herself defending him instinctively. "But you were an adventurer. You did lots of different things, and did them well."

"I was young, without roots or a future," he contradicted her gently. "For the first time I stopped to think about what I'd be like, what I'd be doing five, ten, fifteen years down the road, and I came up with a big fat zip."

"So you decided to be a photographer, just like that?" She was skeptical, though if that had been the case it would be a remarkable success story.

"Actually, I decided to write about what I'd been doing. There's always a market for adventure books. I envisioned myself traveling the world, doing all kinds of interesting things—reenacting ancient voyages across oceans, scaling previously unscaled mountain peaks, crossing the Sahara with two camels and canteens of water . . ."

"Did you do any of those things?"

"Nope."

"Then . . . you wrote about things you'd already done?"

"Nope." When she frowned, he explained. "I couldn't write for beans. I tried, Lord how I tried. I sat for hours and hours with blank paper in front of me, finally scribbling something down, then crossing it out and crumbling the sheet into a ball." He arched a brow in self-mockery. "I got pretty good at hitting the wastebasket on the first try."

A small smile touched her lips. "Oh."

"But—" he held up a finger "—it wasn't a total waste. Y'see, I'd pictured my articles in something like *National Geographic*, and of course there were going to be gorgeous photographs accompanying the text, and who better to take them than me, since I was there—actually I was in New Mexico at the time, on an archaeological dig."

"Had you ever used a camera before?"

"No, but that didn't stop me. It was an adventure in and of itself. I bought a used camera, got a few books, read up on what I had to do, and . . . click. Literally and figuratively."

He stopped talking and sat back. Marni felt as though she'd been left dangling. "And . . . ?"

"And what?"

"What happened? Did you sell those first pictures?"

"Not to *National Geographic*."

"But you did sell them?"

"Uh-huh."

Again she waited. He was smiling, but he made no attempt to go on. She remembered that he'd been that way fourteen years ago, too. When she'd asked him about the things he'd done, there'd been a quiet smugness to him. He'd held things back until she'd specifically asked, and when his stories came out they were like a well-earned prize. In his way he'd manipulated her, forcing her to show her cards. Perhaps he was manipulating her now. But she didn't care.

Hadn't he been the one to say that they should get to know each other?

"Okay," she said. "You photographed a dig in New Mexico and sold the pictures to a magazine. But photographing a dig is a far cry from photographing some of the world's most famous personalities. How did it happen? How did you switch from photographing arrowheads, or whatever, to photographing *head* heads?"

He chuckled. "Poetically put, if I don't say so myself. You should be the writer, Marni. You could write. I could photograph."

"I've already got a full-time job, thank you. Come on, Web. When did you get your first break?"

Just then the wine steward arrived with an ice bucket. He uncorked the wine, poured a taste for Web, then at Web's nod filled both of their glasses.

Web's thoughts weren't on the wine, but on the fact that he was thoroughly enjoying himself. The Marni sitting across from him now was so like the Marni he'd known fourteen years before that he couldn't help but smile in wonder. She was curious. She'd always been curious. She couldn't help herself, and he'd been counting on that. Personalities didn't change. Time and circumstances modified them, perhaps, but they never fully changed.

"Web . . . ?" she prodded. "How did it happen?"

"Actually it was on that same trip. The dig I was working at was being used as the backdrop for a movie. Given the way I always had with people—" he winked, and she should have been angry but instead felt a delicious curling in her stomach "—I got myself into the middle of the movie set and started snapping away."

"Don't tell me that those first shots sold?"

"I won't. They were awful. I mean, they had potential. I liked the expressions I caught, the emotions, and I found

photographing people much more exciting than photographing arrowheads or whatever. Technically I had a lot
to learn, though, so I signed on with a photographer in L.A.
After six months, I went out on my own."

"Six months? That's all? It takes years for most photographers to develop sufficient skill to do what you do and do
it right."

"I didn't have years. I felt I'd already wasted too many,
and I needed to earn money. There's that small matter of
having a roof over your head and food enough to keep your
body going, not to mention the larger matter of equipment
and a studio. I started modestly, shooting outside mostly,
working my buns off, turning every cent I could back into
better equipment. I used what I'd learned apprenticing as a
base, and picked up more as I went along. I read. I talked
with other photographers. I studied the work of the masters and poured through magazine after magazine to see
what the market wanted and needed. I did portfolios for
models and actors and actresses, and things seemed to
mushroom from there."

"Did you have a long-range goal?"

"New York. Cover work. Independence, within limits."

"Then you've made it," she declared, unaware of the pride
that lit her eyes. Web wasn't unaware of it though, and it
gave him unbelievable pleasure.

"I suppose you could say that," he returned softly.
"There's always more I want to do, and the field keeps pace
with changes in fashion. The real challenge is in making my
work different from the others. I want my pictures to have
a unique look and feel. I guess I need that more than anything—knowing I'll have left an indelible mark behind."

"Are you going somewhere?" she teased.

There was sadness in his smile. "We're all mortal. I think about that a lot. At the rate I'm going, my work will be just about all I do leave behind."

"You never married." It was a statement, offered softly, with a hint of timidness.

"I've been too busy.... What about you?"

"The same."

The waiter chose that moment to appear with their food, and they lapsed into silence for a time as they ate.

"Funny," Web said at last, "I'd really pictured you with a husband and kids and a big, beautiful home in the country."

She gave a sad laugh. "So had I."

"Dreams gone awry, or simply deferred?"

She pondered that for a minute. "I really don't know. I've been so caught up with running the business that it seems there isn't time for much else."

"You must do things for fun."

"I do . . . now and again." She stopped pushing the Parisienne potatoes around her plate and put down her fork. "What about you? Are you still working as hard as you did at first?"

"I'm working as hard, but the focus is different. I can concentrate on the creative end and leave the rest to assistants. I have specialists for my finish work, and even though I'm more often than not at their shoulders, approving everything before it leaves the studio, I do have more free time. I try to take weekends completely off."

"What do you do then?"

He shrugged. "Mostly I go to Vermont. I have a small place there. In the winter I ski. In the summer I swim."

"Sounds heavenly," she said, meaning it.

"Don't you still go to Camden?"

She straightened, and the look of pleasure faded from her face. "My parents still do. It's an institution with them. Me, well, I don't enjoy it the way I used to. Sometimes staying here in New York for the summer is a vacation in itself." She gave a dry laugh. "Everyone else is gone. It's quieter."

"You always did like peace and quiet," he said, remembering that day so long ago when they'd gone mountain climbing.

Marni remembered, too. Her gaze grew momentarily lost in his, lost in the memory of that happy, carefree time. It was with great effort that she finally looked away. She took a deep breath. "Anyway, I try to take an extra day or two when I'm off somewhere on business—you know, relax in a different place to shake off the tension."

"Alone?"

"Usually."

"Then there's no special man?"

"No."

"You must date?"

"Not unless I'm inspired, and I'm rarely inspired." Just then her eye was caught by a couple very clearly approaching their table. Following her gaze, Web turned around. He pushed his chair back, stood and extended his hand to the man.

"How are you, Frank?"

The newcomer added a gentle shoulder slap to the handshake. "Not bad."

Web enclosed the woman's hand in his, then leaned forward and kissed her cheek. "Maggie, you're looking wonderful. Frank, Maggie, I'd like you to meet Marni Lange. Marni, these are the Kozols."

Marni barely had time to shake hands with each before Frank was studying her, tapping his lip. "Marni Lange...of the Lange Corporation?"

She cast a skittish glance at Web, then nodded.

"I knew your father once upon a time," Frank went on. "Gee, I haven't seen him in years."

"He's retired now," she offered gracefully, though mention of her father in Web's presence made her uneasy.

"Is he well? And your mother?"

"They're both fine, thank you."

Maggie had come around the table to more easily chat with her. "Frank was with Eastern Engineering then, though he went out on his own ten years ago." She looked over to find her husband engrossed in an animated discussion with Web, and she smiled indulgently. "You'll have to excuse him. I know it's rude for us to barge in on your dinner this way, but he's so fond of Brian that he simply had to stop in and say hello."

Marni smiled. "It's perfectly all right. Have you known . . . Brian long?"

"Several years. Our daughter is—was—a model. When she first went to Brian to be photographed, she was pretty confused. He was wonderful. I really think that if it hadn't been for him, she would have ended up in a sorry state. She's married now and just had her first child." Maggie beamed. "The baby's a jewel."

"Boy...girl?" Out of the corner of her eye, Marni saw Web standing with one hand in his trousers pocket. He looked thoroughly in command, totally at ease and very handsome. She realized that she was proud to be with him.

"A boy. Christopher James. He's absolutely precious."

Marni retrained her focus on Maggie. "And you're enjoying him. Do they live close by?"

"In Washington. We've been down several times—"

"Come on, sweetheart," Frank cut in. "The car's waiting, and these folks don't need us taking any more of their time."

Maggie turned briefly back to Marni. "It was lovely meeting you." Then she gave Web a kiss and let her husband guide her off.

"Sorry about that," Web murmured, sitting down again. He pulled his chair closer to the table.

"Don't apologize." It was the first time she'd ever met any friends of Web's. "They seemed lovely. Maggie was mentioning her daughter. They're both in your debt, I take it."

He shrugged. "She was a sweet kid who was lost in the rat race of modeling. Maggie and Frank say that she was 'confused,' and she was, but she was also on drugs and she was practically anorexic."

"Isn't that true of lots of models?"

"Mmm, but it was particularly sad with Sara. She had a good home. Her folks are loaded. I'm not sure she even wanted to model in the first place, but she had the looks and the style, and she somehow got snagged. If she hadn't gotten out when she did, she'd probably be dead by now."

Marni winced. "What did you do for her?"

He grew more thoughtful. "Talked, mostly. I took the pictures and made sure they were stupendous. Then I tried to convince her that she'd hit the top and ought to retire."

"And just like that she did?"

"Not . . . exactly. I showed her my morgue book."

"Morgue book?"

"Mmm. I keep files on everyone I've photographed, with a follow-up on each. I have a special folder—pictures of people who made it big, then plummeted. When I'm feeling sorry for myself about one thing or another, I take it out, and it makes me grateful for what I've got. I don't show it to many people, but it gave Sara something to think about. She came back to see me often after that, and I finally convinced her to see a psychiatrist. Maggie and Frank are terrific, but Sara was their daughter, and the thought that she'd actually need a psychiatrist disturbed them."

"But it worked."

"It helped. Mostly what helped was meeting her husband. He's a rock, a lawyer with the Justice Department, and he's crazy about her. He supported her completely when she decided to go back to school to get the degree she missed out on when she began modeling." He cleared his throat meaningfully. "I think the baby has interrupted that now, but Sara knows she can go back whenever she's ready."

"That's a lovely story," Marni said with a smile. "I'll bet you have lots of others about people you've photographed." She propped her elbow on the table and set her chin in her palm. "Tell me some."

For the next hour, he did just that. There was a modesty to him, and she had to coax him on from time to time, but when he got going his tales fascinated her every bit as much as those he'd told fourteen years before had done. The years evaporated. She listened, enthralled, thinking how exciting his life was and how he was fully in control of it.

By the time they'd finished their second cup of coffee, they'd fallen silent and were simply looking at each other. Their communication continued, but on a different level, one in which Marni was too engrossed to analyze.

"Just like old times," Web said quietly.

She nodded and smiled almost shyly. "I could sit listening to you for hours. You were always so different from other people. You had such a wealth of experience to draw on. You still do."

"You've got experience of your own—"

"But not as exciting. Or maybe I just take it for granted. Do you ever do that?"

"I wish I could. If I start taking things for granted, I'll stop growing, and if that happens I'll never make it the way I want to."

"That means a lot to you...making it." So different from how he'd been, she mused. Then again, perhaps he'd only defined success differently fourteen years ago.

"Everyone wants success. Don't you? Isn't that why you pour so much of yourself into the business?"

She didn't answer him immediately. Her feelings were torn. Yes, she wanted to be successful as president of the Lange Corporation, but for reasons she didn't want to think about, much less discuss. "I guess," she said finally.

"You don't sound sure."

She forced herself to perk up. "I'm sure."

"But there was something else you were thinking about just now. What was it, Marni?"

She smiled and shook her head. "Nothing. It was really nothing. I think I'm just tired. It's been a long day."

"And a trying one."

"Yes," she whispered.

Not wanting to push her too far, Web didn't argue. He'd done most of the talking during dinner, and though there were still many things he wanted to know about Marni, many things he wanted to discuss with her, he felt relatively satisfied with what he'd accomplished. He'd wanted to tell her about his work, and he had. He'd wanted to give her a glimpse of the man he was now, and he had. He'd wanted to give her something to think about besides the past, and he had. He was determined to make her trust him again. Tonight had simply been the first down payment on that particular mortgage. There would be time enough in the future to make more headway, he mused as he dug into his pocket to settle the bill. There would be time. He'd make time. He wasn't sure what he wanted in the long run from

Marni, but he did know that their relationship had been left suspended fourteen years ago, and that it needed to be settled one way or another.

They hit the cold night air the instant they left the restaurant. Marni bundled her coat around her more snugly, and when Web drew her back into the shelter of the doorway and threw his arm around her shoulder while they waited for the car, she didn't resist. He was large, warm and strong. He'd always been large, warm and strong.

For an instant she closed her eyes and pretended that that summer hadn't ended as it had. It was a sweet, sweet dream, and her senses filled to brimming with the taste, the touch, the smell of him. She loved Web. Her body tingled from his closeness. They were on their way to a secret rendezvous where he'd make the rest of the world disappear and lift her onto a plane of sheer bliss.

"Here we go," he murmured softly.

She began to tremble.

"Marni?"

Web was squeezing her shoulder. She snapped her eyes open and stared.

"The car. It's here."

Stunned, she let herself be guided into the front seat. By the time she realized what had happened, the neon lights of the city were flickering through the windshield as they passed, camouflaging her embarrassment.

Web said nothing. He drove skillfully and at a comfortable pace. When they arrived at her building, he left his keys with the doorman and rode the elevator with her to her door. There he took her own keys, released the lock, then stood back while she deactivated the burglar alarm.

With the door partially open, she raised her eyes to his. "Thank you, Web. I've . . . this was nice."

"I thought so." He smiled so gently that her heart turned over. "You're really something to be with."

"I'm not. You carried most of the evening."

He winked. "I was inspired."

Her limbs turned to jelly and did nothing by way of solidifying when he put a light hand on her shoulder. His expression grew more serious, almost troubled.

"Marni, about that cover—"

"Shhhh." She put an impulsive finger on his lips to stem the words, then wished she hadn't because the texture of his mouth, its warmth, was like fire. She snatched her hand away and dropped her gaze to his tie. It was textured, too, but of silk, and its smooth-flowing stripes of navy, gray and mauve were serene, soothing. "Please," she whispered. "Let's not argue about that again."

"I still want to do it. Don't you think it would be easier for you now?"

"I . . . I don't know."

"Will you think about it at least? We couldn't try it again until early next week anyway. Maybe by then you'll be feeling more comfortable."

She dipped her head lower. "I don't know."

"Marni?"

She squeezed her eyes shut, knowing she should slip through her door and lock it tight, but was unable to move. When he curved one long forefinger under her chin and tipped it up, she resisted. He simply applied more pressure until at last she met his gaze.

"It's still there," he whispered. "You know that, don't you?"

Eyes large and frightened, she nodded.

"Do we have to fight it?"

"I'm not ready." She was whispering, too, not out of choice, but because she couldn't seem to produce anything louder. Her heart was pounding, its beat reverberating through her limbs. "I don't know if I'm . . . ready for this. I suffered so . . . last time . . ."

He was stroking her cheek with the back of his hand, a hand that had once known every inch of her in the most intimate detail. His blue eyes were clouded. "I suffered, too. You don't know. I suffered, too, Marni. Do you think I want to go through that again?"

She swallowed hard, then shook her head.

"I wouldn't suggest something I felt would hurt either of us."

"What *are* you suggesting?"

"Friday night. See me Friday night. There's a party I have to go to, make a quick appearance at. I'd like you to come with me, then we can take off and do something—dinner, a movie, a ride through the park, I don't care what, but I have to see you again."

"Something's screwed up here. I was always the one to do the chasing."

"Because I was arrogant and cocksure, and so caught up in playing the role of the carefree bachelor that I didn't know any better." His thumb skated lightly over her lips. "I'm tired of playing, Marni. I'm too old for that now. I want to see you again. I *have* to see you again. . . . How about it? Friday night?"

"I can't promise you anything about the picture."

"Friday night. No business, just fun. Please?"

If fourteen years ago anyone had told Marni that Web would be pleading with her to see him, she would never have believed it. If thirteen years ago, ten years ago, five or even one year ago anyone had told Marni that she'd *be* seeing him again, she would never have believed it.

"Yes," she said softly, knowing that there was no other choice she could possibly make. Web did something to her.

He'd *always* done something to her. He made her feel things she'd never felt with another man. Shock, pain, shimmering physical awareness...she was alive. That, in itself, was a precious gift.

4

THE PARTY WAS unbelievably raucous. Pop music throbbed through the air at ear-splitting decibels, aided and abetted by the glare of brightly colored floodlights and the sea of bodies contorting every which way in a tempest of unleashed energy.

The host was a rock video producer whom Web had met several months before through a mutual subject of their respective lenses. The guest list ran the gamut from actors to singers to musicians to technicians.

Marni could barely distinguish one garishly lit face, one outrageously garbed body from another, and she would have felt lost had it not been for the umbilical cord of Web's arm. He introduced her to those he knew and joined her in greeting others he was meeting for the first time. Marni couldn't say that it was the most intellectually stimulating group she'd ever encountered, but then her own mind could barely function amid the pulsating hubbub of activity.

In hindsight, though, it was an educational hour that she spent with Web at the party. She learned that he was well-known, well-liked and held slightly in awe. She learned that he didn't play kissy-and-huggy-and-isn't-this-a-*super*-party, but maintained his dignity while appearing fully congenial and at ease. She learned that he disliked indiscriminate drinking and avoided the coke corner like the plague, that he hated Twisted Sister, abided Prince, admired Springsteen, and that he was not much more of a dancer than she was.

"I think I'm getting a migraine," he finally yelled at her over the din. "Come on. Let's get out of here." He tugged her by the hand, leading her first for their coats, then out the door. Once in the lobby, where the music was little more than a dull vibration, he leaned back against the wall. Their coats were slung over his shoulder. He hadn't released her hand once. "Sorry about that," he said, tipping his head sideways against the stucco wall to look at her. "I hadn't realized it'd be so wild. Well, maybe I had, but I promised Malcolm I'd come. Are you still with me?"

She, too, was braced against the wall, savoring their escape. She gave his hand a squeeze and smiled. "A little wilted, but I'm still here."

"I want you to know that these aren't really my friends. I mean, Malcolm is, and I know enough of the others, but I don't usually hang around with them in my free time. Even if I did it'd be one at a time and in a quieter setting, but I really do have other, more reputable friends.... What are you laughing at?"

"You. You were so confident back there, but all of a sudden you're like a little boy, all nervous and apologetic." She punctuated her words with a chiding headshake, but she was grinning. "I'm not your mother, Web. And I'm not here to stand in judgment on your friends and acquaintances."

"I know, but . . . why is it I suspect that your friends are a little more . . . dignified?"

She grimaced. "Maybe because I'm the staid president of a staid corporation."

"Hey, I'm not knocking it.... What *are* your friends like?"

"Oh . . . diverse. Quieter, I guess." She paused pensively. "It's strange. When I think back to being a teenager, to the group I was with then, I remember irreverent parties and a general law-unto-ourselves attitude."

"You were never really that way."

"No, but I was on the fringe of it. When I think of what those same people, even the most rebellious ones, are doing now, I have to laugh. They're conventional, establishment all the way. Oh, they like a good time, and by and large they've got plenty of money to spend on one, but they seem to have outgrown that wildness they so prided themselves on."

"You say 'they.' You don't identify with them?"

She plucked at the folds of the chic overblouse she'd worn with her stirrup pants. "It wasn't that I outgrew it. I was shocked into leaving it behind. Somehow I lost a taste for it after... after..."

"After Ethan died," he finished for her in a sober voice. When she didn't reply, he took her coat from his shoulder. "Come on," he said gently. "Let's take a walk."

Without raising her head, she slipped her arms into the sleeves of the coat and buttoned it up, then let Web take her hand and lead her into the February night. The party had been in SoHo at the lower end of Manhattan. They'd taxied there, but a slow walk back uptown was what they both needed.

"You still miss him, don't you?" Web asked.

The air was cold, numbing her just enough to enable her to talk of Ethan. "I adored him. There were eight years between us, and it wasn't as though we were close in the sense of baring our souls to each other. But we shared a special something. Yes, I miss him."

Web wrapped his arm around her shoulders and drew her close as they walked. "He would have been president of Lange, wouldn't he?"

"Yes."

"You took over in his place."

"My parents needed someone."

"What about your sister . . . Tanya?"

Marni's laugh was brittle. "Tanya is hopeless. She ran in the opposite direction when she thought she might have to do something with the business. Not that Dad would have asked her. Maybe it was because he *didn't* ask her that she was so negative about it. She never did get her degree. She flunked out of two different colleges and finally gave up on the whole thing."

"What is she doing now?"

"Oh, she's here in New York. She's been through two husbands and is looking around for a third. She's got alimony enough to keep her living in style, so she spends her days shopping and her nights partying."

"Not *your* cup of tea."

"Not . . . quite."

"Were you ever close, you and Tanya?"

"Not really. We fought all the time as kids, you know, bickered like all siblings do. When I read things about sibling placement, about how the middle child is supposed to be the mediator, I have to laugh. Tanya was the *instigator*. It's like she felt lost between Ethan and me, and had to go out of her way to exert herself. I was some kind of threat to her—don't ask me why. She's prettier, more outgoing. And she can dance." They both chuckled. "But she always seemed to think that I had something she didn't, or that I was going to get something better than what she did."

"She was two years older than you?"

"Mmmm."

"Maybe she resented your arrival. If Ethan was seven when she was born, and she was the first girl, she was probably pampered for those first two years of her life. Your birth upset the applecart."

Marni sighed. "Whatever, it didn't—doesn't—make for a comfortable relationship. We see each other at family events, and run into each other accidentally from time to time, but we rarely talk on the phone and we never go out of our way to spend time together. It's sad, when you think of it." She looked up at Web. "You must think it's pathetic . . . being an only child and all."

"I wasn't an only child."

Her eyes widened. "No? But I thought . . . you never mentioned any family, and I always assumed you didn't have any!"

His lips twitched. "Just hatched from a shell and took off, eh?"

"You know what I mean. What *do* you have, Web? Tell me."

"I have a brother. Actually a half brother. He's four years younger than me."

"Do you ever see him?"

"We work together. He's my business manager, or agent, or financial advisor, or whatever you want to call it. Lee Fitzgerald. He was there Tuesday morning. . .but you don't remember much of that, do you?"

She eyed him shamefacedly. "I wasn't exactly at my best Tuesday morning."

"You wouldn't have had any way of knowing he was my brother. We don't look at all alike. But he's a nice guy, and very capable."

Marni was remembering what Web had said that Tuesday morning, in a moment of anger, about his being a bastard. "The name Webster?"

"Was my mother's maiden name."

"Did you ever know your father?"

"Nope. It was a one-night stand. He was married."

"Do you ever . . . wonder about him?"

He caressed her shoulder through the thickness of her coat as though he needed that small reassurance of her presence. Though his tone was light, devoid of bitterness, almost factual, Marni suspected that he regretted the circumstances of his conception.

"I wouldn't be human if I didn't. I used to do it a lot when I was a kid—wonder who he was, what he looked like, where he lived, whether he'd like me. I can almost empathize with Tanya. I spent all those years wandering, traveling, never staying in one place long. Maybe I didn't want to learn that he wasn't looking for me. As long as I kept moving, I had that illusion that he might be looking but, of course, couldn't find me. Pretty dumb, huh? He doesn't even know I exist."

Marni's heart ached for him. "Your mother never told him?"

"My mother never *saw* him, not after that one night. She knew his name, but he was a salesman from somewhere or other. She didn't know where. And she knew he was married, so she didn't bother. She married my stepfather when I was two. He wasn't a bad sort as stepfathers go."

They turned onto Fifth Avenue, walking comfortably in step with each other. "Is your mother still living?"

"She died several years ago."

"I'm sorry, Web," Marni said, feeling all the more guilty about the times she'd resented her own parents. At least they were alive. If she had a problem, she had somewhere to run. "Do you still wonder about your father?"

"Nah. I reached a point when settling down meant more than running away from the fact that he didn't know about me. I decided I wanted to do something, be something. I'm proud of what I've become."

"You should be," she said softly, holding his gaze for a minute, until the intensity of its soul-reach made her look away.

They walked silently for a few blocks, their way lit frequently by storefront lights or the headlights of cars whipping through the city night. The sound of motors, revving, slowing, filled the air, along with the occasional honk of a horn or the squeal of brakes or the whir of tires.

"What about you, Marni? I know what you've become, but what would you have done if . . . things had been different. I knew you wanted a college degree, but you hadn't said much more than that. Had you always wanted to join the corporation?"

"I hadn't thought that far. Business, a career—they were the last things on my mind—" her voice lowered "—until Ethan died. I grew up pretty fast then."

"Why? I mean, you were only seventeen."

"Ethan had already started working, and I knew he was being groomed to take over Dad's place one day. It wasn't like I wanted the presidency per se, but my father needed someone, and it seemed right that I should give it a try."

"Did you go to Wellesley after all?"

"Mmmm. I did pretty lousy my first term. I was still pretty upset. But after that I was able to settle down. I got my M.B.A. at Columbia, and joined the corporation from there."

"Are you sorry? Do you ever wish you were doing something else?"

"I wish Ethan were here to be president, but given that he's not, I really can't complain. I do have an aptitude for business. I think I'm good at what I do. There's challenge to the work, and a sense of power because the corporation is profitable and I'm free to venture into new things."

"Like *Class*."

"Like *Class*."

They turned from Fifth Avenue onto a side street that was darker and more deserted. Marni couldn't remember the last time she'd walked through the city like this at night. She'd always been too intent on getting from one place to another, via cab or car or limousine, to think of walking. Yet, now it was calming, therapeutic, really quite nice. Of course, it helped that Web was with her. Talking with him was easy. He made her think about things—like Ethan—and doing so brought less pain than she'd have expected. Ethan was gone; she couldn't bring him back. But Web was here.

He'd never take the place of her brother; for that matter, she couldn't even *think* of Web as a brother. It wasn't a brother she wanted anyway. She wasn't sure just what she did want from Web—she hadn't thought that far. But his presence had an odd kind of continuity to it. Tonight, even Tuesday night when he'd taken her to dinner, she'd felt an inner excitement she hadn't experienced since she'd been seventeen years old. She felt good being with him—proud of what he was, how he looked, how he looked at *her*—and she felt infinitely safe, protected with his arm around her and his sturdy body so close.

Just then, a muffled cry came from the dark alleyway they'd just passed. They stopped and looked at each other, and their eyes grew wider when the sound came again. Suddenly Web was moving, pressing Marni into the alcove of a storefront. "Play dead," he whispered, then turned and ran back toward the alley. He'd barely reached its mouth when a body barreled into him, sending him sprawling, but only for an instant. Acting reflexively, he was on his feet and after the man, who was surprisingly smaller and slower than he.

But smaller and slower was one thing. When he dragged the nameless fugitive to the ground nearly halfway down the block, he found that he was no match for the shiny switchblade that connected with his left hand. Shards of pain splintered through him, and he recoiled, clutching his hand. He had no aspirations to be a hero or a martyr. Letting the man go, he ran back to where he'd left Marni. She was gone.

"Maaaarni!" he yelled, terrified for the first time.

"In here, Web! The alley!"

He swore, then dashed into the alley, skidding to a halt and coming down on his haunches beside her. She was supporting a young woman who was gasping for air.

"It's all right," Marni was saying softly but tightly. "It's all right. He's gone."

"Did he rape her?" Web asked Marni. He could see that the woman's clothes were torn.

She shook her head. "Our passing must have scared him off. He took her wallet. That's about it."

Web put a hand on the woman's quivering arm. "I'm going to get the police. Stay with Marni until I get back."

Her answering nod was nearly imperceptible amid her trembling, but Marni doubted she could have moved if she'd wanted to.

Web dashed back to the street, wondering where the traffic was when he wanted it. He ran to the corner of Fifth Avenue, intent on hailing some help. Cars whizzed by without pausing. The cabs were all occupied, so they didn't bother to stop. And there wasn't a policeman or a cruiser in sight. Spotting a pay phone, he dug into his pocket for a quarter, quickly called in the alarm, then raced back to the alley.

Marni was where he'd left her, still cradling the woman. Frightened, she looked up at him. "He must have hurt her. She has blood on her sleeve, but I don't know where it's coming from."

"It's mine," Web said, crouching down again. He was feeling a little dizzy. Both of his hands were covered with blood, one from holding the other. Tugging the scarf from around his neck, he wound it tightly around his left hand.

"My God, Web!" Marni whispered. Her heart, racing already, began to slam against her ribs. "What *happened*?"

"He had a knife. Lucky he used it on me, not her."

"But your hand—"

"It'll be all right."

The woman in Marni's arms began to cry. "I'm sorry...it's my fault. I shouldn't have . . . been walking alone. . . ."

Marni smoothed matted strands of hair from the young woman's cheeks. She couldn't have been more than twenty-two or twenty-three, was thin and not terribly attractive. Yes, she should have known better, but that was water over the dam. "Shhhh. It's all right. The police will be here soon." She raised questioning eyes to Web, who nodded. Then she worriedly eyed his hand.

"It's okay," he assured her softly. He turned to the woman who'd been assaulted. "What's your name, honey?"

"Denise . . . Denise LaVecque."

"You're going to be just fine, Denise. The police will be along shortly." As though on cue, a distant siren grew louder. "They're going to want to know everything you can remember about the man who attacked you."

"I . . . I can't remember much. It was dark. He just . . . jumped out . . ."

"Anything you can remember will be a help to them."

The siren neared. It hit Marni that Denise wasn't the only one in for a long night. "They'll want to know everything you remember, too," she told Web.

He closed his eyes for a minute, frowning. His hand was beginning to throb. He wasn't sure if his wool scarf had been the best thing to wrap around it, but he'd needed to hide its condition from Marni—and from himself, if the truth were told. "I know."

Marni's hand on his cheek brought his eyes back open. "Are you really okay?" she whispered tremulously.

He gave a wan smile and nodded.

The siren rounded the corner and died at the same time a glaring flash of blue and white intruded on the darkness of the alley. It was a welcome intrusion.

The next few minutes passed by in a whir for Marni. A second police car joined the first, with four of New York's finest offering their slightly belated aid, asking question after question, searching the alley for anything Denise's assailant may have dropped, finally bundling Denise off in one car, Web and Marni in another. Marni wasn't sure what their plans were for Denise, but she was vocal in her insistence that Web be taken to a hospital before he answered any further questions.

The drive there was a largely silent one. Marni held Web's good hand tightly, worriedly glancing at him from time to time.

"It's just a cut," he murmured when he intercepted one such glance, but his head was lying back against the seat and the night could hide neither his pallor nor the blood seeping through the thickness of his scarf.

"My hero," was her retort, but it was more gentle than chiding, more admiring than censorious. She suspected that he'd acted on sheer instinct in chasing after the man who'd attacked Denise, and in a city notorious for its avoidance of involvement in such situations she deeply respected what Web had done. Of course, tangling with a switchblade hadn't been too swift . . .

The nurse at the emergency room desk immediately took Web to a cubicle, but when she suggested that Marni might want to wait outside, Marni firmly shook her head. She continued to hold Web's hand tightly, releasing it only to help him out of his coat and to roll up his sleeve. He sat on the examining table with his legs hanging down one side; she sat with her legs hanging down the other, her elbow hooked with his, her eyes over her shoulder focusing past him to his left hand, which a doctor was carefully unwrapping.

She didn't move from where she sat. Her arm tightened periodically around Web's as the doctor cleaned the knife wound, then examined it to see the extent of the damage. When Web winced, so did she. When he grunted at a particularly painful probe, she moaned.

"You okay?" he asked her at one point. The doctor had just announced that the tendon in his baby finger had been severed and that it would take a while to heal, what with stitches and all.

"I'm okay," she told Web. "You're the one who's sweating."

He grinned peakedly. "It hurts like hell."

Feeling utterly helpless, she turned on the doctor. "He's in pain. Can't you help—"

"Marni," Web interrupted, "it's only my hand."

"But the pain's probably shooting up your arm, and don't you tell me it isn't!" She felt it herself, through her hand, her arm, her entire body. Again she accosted the doctor. "Aren't you going to anesthetize him or something?"

The doctor gave her an understanding smile. "Just his hand. Right now." He took the needle that the nurse assisting him had suddenly produced, and Marni did look away then, but only until Web rubbed his cheek against her hair.

"You can open your eyes now," he said softly, a hint of amusement in his tone. "It's all done."

What was done was the anesthetizing. The gash, which cut through his baby finger and continued across his palm, was as angry-looking as ever.

"You may think this is funny, Brian Webster," she scolded in a hoarse whisper, "but I don't. Who knows what filthy germs were on that knife, or how you're going to handle a camera with one hand immobilized."

"Do you think I'm not worried about those same things?" he asked gently.

"No need to worry, Mr. Webster," the doctor interjected. "I'll give you a shot to counter whatever may have been on the knife, and as for your work, it's just your pinkie that will be in a splint. Between your thumb and the first two fingers of that left hand, you should be able to manage your camera. Maybe a little awkwardly at first, but you'll adapt."

"See?" Web said to Marni. "I'll adapt."

Marni didn't reply. She felt guilty for having badgered him, but she was worried and upset, and she'd had to let off the tension somehow. Turning her gaze back to his wound, which the doctor was beginning to stitch, she slid her free arm over Web's shoulder. He reached up, grasped her hand and wove his fingers through hers.

"Does it hurt?" she whispered.

He, too, was closely following the doctor's work, but he managed to shake his head. "Don't feel a thing."

"I'm glad one of us doesn't," she quipped dryly, and he chuckled.

Millimeter by millimeter the doctor closed the gash. Once, riding a wave of momentary fatigue, Marni pressed her face to the crook of Web's neck. He tipped his head to hold her there, finding intense comfort in the closeness.

When the repair work was done, the doctor splinted the finger and bandaged the hand. He gave Web the shot he'd promised, plus a small envelope with painkillers that he claimed Web might need as soon as the local anesthetic wore off. Marni would have liked nothing more than to take him home at that point, but the police were waiting just beyond the cubicle to take them to the station.

"Can't this be done tomorrow?" Marni asked softly. "I think he should be resting."

Web squeezed her hand. "It's okay. If we go now, we'll get it over with. The sooner the better, before the numbness wears off. Besides, I'm not sure I want to spend my Saturday poring through mug shots."

She would have argued further, but she realized he had a point. "You'll tell me if you start feeling lousy?"

"I think you'll know," he returned, arching one dark brow. She hadn't let go of him for a minute, and he loved it. Barely five minutes had gone by when she hadn't looked at his face for signs of discomfort or asked how he felt, and he loved it. He'd never been the object of such concern in his life. And he loved it.

He didn't love wading through page after page of mug shots in search of the man he'd seen and chased, but the police were insistent, and he knew it was necessary. He particularly didn't love it when the wee hours of the morning approached and they were still at it, he and Marni. His hand was beginning to ache again, and as the minutes passed, his head was, too. He new that Marni had to be totally exhausted, and while he wanted to send her home, he also needed her by his side.

"Nothing," he said wearily when the last of the books were closed. "I'm sorry, but I don't think the man I saw tonight is here."

The officer who had been working with them rose from his perch on the corner of the desk and took the book from Web. "Hit and run. They're the damnedest ones to catch. May have been wearing a wig, or have shaved off a mustache. May not have any previous record, if you can believe that."

Marni, for one, was ready to believe anything the man said, if only to secure her and Web's release. Not only was she tired, but the events of the night had begun to take an emotional toll. She was feeling distinctly shaky.

"Is there anything else we have to do now?" she asked fearfully.

"Nope. I've got your statements, and I know where to reach you if we come up with anything."

Web was slipping his coat on. He didn't bother to put his left arm into the sleeve. It wasn't worth the effort. "Do you think you will?"

"Nope."

Web sighed. "Well, if you need us . . ."

The officer nodded, then stood aside, and Web and Marni wound their way through the maze of desks, doorways and stairs to the clear, cold air outside. They headed straight for a waiting taxi.

"I'd better get you home," he murmured, opening the door for Marni. As she slid in, she leaned forward and gave the cabbie Web's address. Web didn't realize what she'd done until they pulled up outside his riverfront building, at which point he was dismayed. "I can't send you home alone in a cab," he protested. "Not after what happened tonight."

Some of her spunk had returned. "I have no intention of going home alone, *especially* after what happened tonight. Come on, big guy." She was shoving him out the door. "We could both use a drink."

He was paying the cabbie when she climbed out herself. She was the one to put her arm around his waist and urge him into the building. "This is not...what...I'd planned," he growled, disgusted when he looked back on an evening that was supposed to have been so pleasant. "I never should have taken you to that party. If we hadn't gone, we wouldn't have been walking down that street—"

"And that poor girl would have been raped." Marni pressed the elevator button. The door slid open instantly, and she tugged him inside. "What ifs aren't any good—I learned that a long time ago. The facts are that we did go to the party, that we were walking down that street, that we managed to deter a vicious crime, that your hand is all cut up and that we're both bleary-eyed right about now." The elevator began its ascent. "I'm exhausted, but I'm afraid to close my eyes because I'll see either that dark alleyway, that girl, or your poor hand. . . . How is it?"

"It's there."

"You wouldn't take one of the painkillers while we were at the police station. Will you take one now?"

"A couple of aspirin'll do the trick."

He ferreted his keys from his pocket and had them waiting when the elevator opened. Moments later they'd passed through the studio, climbed the spiral staircase and were in his living room. He went straight to the bar, tipped a bottle into each of two glasses without thought to either ice or water, took a long drink from his glass, then handed the other to Marni.

"Come. Sit with me." He moved to the sofa, kicked off his loafers and sank down, stretching out his legs and leaning his head back.

"Where's the aspirin?" Marni asked softly.

"Medicine chest. Down the hall, through the bedroom to the bathroom."

She found her way easily, so intent on getting something into Web that she saw nothing of the rest of his apartment but the inside of the medicine chest above the sink. When she returned, he downed the aspirin with another drink from his glass. She sat facing him on the sofa, her elbow braced on the sofa back.

"You look awful," she whispered.

He didn't open his eyes. "I've felt better."

"Maybe you should lie down."

"I am." He was sprawled backward, his lean body molded to the cushions.

"In bed. Wouldn't you be more comfortable there?"

"Soon."

Very gently, she lifted his injured hand and put it in her lap. She wanted to soothe him, to do something to help, but she wasn't sure what would be best. She began to lightly stroke his forearm, and when he didn't complain she continued.

He smirked. "Some night."

"It certainly was an adventure. You were always into them. This is the first one I've taken part in."

"I think I'm getting too old for this. I'm getting too old for lots of things. I should be up in Vermont. It's quieter there."

"Why aren't you? I thought you went up every weekend."

He opened one eye and looked at her. "I wanted to be with you. I didn't think you'd go up there with me." When she said nothing, he closed his eye and returned his head to its original position. "Anyway, I often wait till Saturday morning to drive up. If there's something doing here on a Friday night."

"You can't drive tomorrow! Well, you can, I suppose, but your hand will be sore—"

"Forget my hand." He made a guttural sound. "The way I feel now, I don't think I'm going to be able to drag myself out of bed before noon, and by then it'd be pretty late to get going."

"You'll go next weekend. It'll still be there."

"Mmmm." He lay still for several minutes, then drained his drink in a single swallow.

Marni set her own glass firmly on the coffee table. She took his empty one, put it beside hers, then gently slid her hand under his neck. "Come on, Web," she urged softly. "Let me get you to bed."

Very slowly and with some effort he pushed himself up, then stood. His hand was hurting, his whole arm was hurting. For that matter, his entire body felt sore. The aftermath of tension, he told himself. He *was* getting old.

Marni led him directly to the bed. The king-sized mattress sat on a platform of dark wood that matched a modern highboy and a second, lower chest of drawers. A plush navy carpet covered the floor. Two chairs of the same contemporary style as those in the living room sat kitty-cornered on one side of the room, between them a low table covered with magazines. Large silk-screen prints hung on the walls, contemporary, almost abstract in style, carrying through the navy, brown and white scheme of the room.

Clear-cut and masculine, like Web, Marni mused as she unbuttoned his shirt and eased it from his shoulders. As soon as it was gone, he turned and whipped the quilt back with his good arm, then stretched out full-length on the bed and threw that same arm across his eyes.

Marni stood where she was with his shirt clutched in her hands and her eyes glued to his bare chest. He was every bit as beautiful as he'd been fourteen years ago, though different in a way that made her heart beat faster than it ever had then. His shoulders were fuller, his skin more weathered. The hair that covered his chest was thicker, more pervasive, even more virile, if that were possible.

Anything was possible, she thought, including the fact that she was as physically attracted to him now as she'd been fourteen years before. Biological magnetism was an amazing thing. Web had been her first, but there'd been others. None of them had turned her on in quite the same way, with quite the intensity Web did.

None of them had stirred feelings of tenderness and caring that Web did either, and he was hurting now, she reminded herself with a jolt. Pushing all other thought aside, she dropped his shirt onto the foot of the bed and came to sit beside him. She unsnapped his jeans and was about to lower the zipper when his arm left his eyes and his hand stilled hers.

"I was...just trying to make you more comfortable," she explained, feeling the sudden flare of those blue eyes on her. "Wouldn't it be better without the jeans?"

"No. I'm fine as I am." Most importantly, he didn't want her to see his leg. She'd had as rough a night as he had, and he didn't feel she was ready to view those particular scars. They were old and well-faded, true, but the memories they'd evoke would be harsh.

Trusting that she wouldn't undress him further, he returned his arm to his eyes and gave a rueful laugh. "Y'know, since I saw you last Tuesday morning, I've been dreaming of having you again. Making love to you...here in my bed. Now here you are and I feel so awful that I don't think I could do a thing even if you were willing."

His words hung in the air, unresolved. Marni couldn't get herself to give the answer she knew Web wanted to hear. There was no doubt in her mind that on the physical level she was willing. Emotionally, well, that was another story. Much as she'd opened up to him since their reunion, much as she'd been able to talk of Ethan more easily than she had in the past, there were still thoughts that she couldn't ignore, raw feelings going back to that summer. Illogical perhaps, but logical ones as well. She knew from experience that one time with Web wouldn't be enough. He'd been an addiction that summer in Maine. She wasn't sure that if she gave in to him, to herself, it would be any different now. And the question would be where they went from there.

"I don't think the time's right for either of us," she said in a near-whisper. "You're right. You're feeling awful. And I feel a little like I've been flattened by a steamroller." She reached for the second pillow and carefully worked it under his bandaged hand. Then she rose from the bed. "I'll just sit over here—"

He raised his arm and looked at her. "You won't leave, will you?"

"No, I won't leave."

"Then why don't you lie down, too. The bed's big enough for both of us."

She wasn't sure she trusted herself that far. "In a little bit," she said, but paused before she sank into the chair. "Can I get you anything?"

Eyes closed, he shook his head. "I think I'll just rest . . ."

When his voice trailed off, she settled into the chair, studying him for a long time until a reflexive twitch of his good hand told her he was asleep. Soon after, her own eyelids drooped, then shut.

Ninety minutes later she came to feeling disoriented and stiff. The first problem was solved when she blinked, looked around the room, then saw Web lying exactly as he had been. The second was solved when she switched off the light, stretched out on the empty half of the bed, drew the quilt over them both and promptly fell asleep.

She awoke several times during the night when Web shifted and groaned. Once she felt his head and found it cool, and when he didn't wake up she lay down again. Her deepest sleep came just before dawn. When next she opened her eyes, the skylit room was bright. The same disorientation possessed her for a minute, but it vanished the minute she turned her head and saw Web.

He was still sleeping. His hair was mussed, and his beard was a dark shadow on his face. But it was his brow, corrugated even in sleep, that drew her gaze. He'd had an uncomfortable night. Silently, she slipped from beneath the sheet and padded to the bathroom for aspirin and water.

He was stirring when she returned, so she sat close by his side, raised him enough to push the aspirin into his mouth and give him a drink, then very gently set his head back down.

"Thanks," he murmured, coming to full awareness. He hadn't been disoriented, since this was his home. Finding Marni sitting beside him, well, that was something else.

"You're welcome. How does it feel...or shouldn't I ask?"

"You shouldn't ask," he drawled, then stretched, twisting his torso. When he settled back, his eyes were on her. "Actually, it's not bad. The discomfort's localized now. It was worse when I was sleeping, because I couldn't pinpoint it and it seemed to be all over." He raised the hand in question and glared at the white gauze. "Helluva big bandage. I'll have to get rid of some of this stuff."

"Don't you dare! If it was put on, it was put on for a reason."

"How am I gonna shower?"

"Hold your hand up in the air out of the spray... or forget the shower and take a bath."

"I never take baths."

She shrugged. "Then take a shower with your hand in the air, and be grateful it's your left hand. If it had been your right, you'd be in *big* trouble."

He ran his palm over the stubble on his jaw. "You've got a point there." His gaze skittered hesitantly to hers. "I must look like something the cat dragged in."

She couldn't have disagreed with him more. He looked a little rough, but all man, every sinewy, stubbly, hairy inch. "You look fine, no, wonderful, given the circumstances." Her voice softened even more. "I've never seen you in the morning this way. We . . . we never spent a full night together."

He smiled in regret, his voice as soft as hers. "So now we've done it, and we haven't even *done* it." He raised his good hand and skimmed a finger over her lips, back and forth, whisper-light. "Do you know, I haven't even kissed you? Lord, I've wanted to, but I didn't know if you wanted it, and it seemed more important to talk."

Marni felt her insides melting. "Fourteen years ago it was the other way around."

"We're older now. Maybe we've got our priorities straight.... But I still want to kiss you." He was stroking her cheek ever so gently, and she'd begun to tremble. "Will you let me?"

"You always had the bluest eyes," she whispered, mesmerized by them, drowning in them. "I could never deny you when you looked at me that way."

"What way?"

"Like you wanted me. Like you knew that maybe it wasn't the smartest thing, but you wanted me anyway. Like there was something about *me* that you wanted, just me."

"There is." He slid his fingers into her hair and urged her head down. "There is, Marni. You're...very...special..." The last was whispered against her lips, the sound vanishing into her mouth, which had opened, and waited, but was waiting no more.

It started gently, a tender reacquaintance, kisses whispered from one mouth to the other in a slow, renewing exchange. For Marni it was a homecoming; there was something about the taste of Web, the texture of his lips, the instinctive way he pleased her that erased the years that had passed. For Web the homecoming was no less true; there was something about the softness of Marni's lips, the way they clung to his, the way her honeyed freshness poured warmly into him that made him forget everything that had come between this and their last kiss.

Familiarly their lips touched and sipped and danced. As it had always done, though, desire soon began to clamor, and whispered kisses were no longer enough. Web's mouth grew more forceful, Marni's demanded in return, and it was fire, hot, sweet fire surging through their veins, singeing all threads of caution.

Eyes closed under the force of sensation, Marni took everything he offered and gave as much in return. His mouth slanted openly against hers, hungrily devouring it. Her mouth fought fiercely for his, possessing it in turn. He ran his tongue along the line of her teeth and beyond; she caressed it with her own, then drew it in deeper. And while his hand wound restlessly through her hair, her own spread feverishly across his chest.

"C'mere," he growled, and swiftly rolled her over him until she was on her back and he was above her. Her neck rested in the crook of his elbow, and it was that elbow that propped him up so he could touch her as she'd done him.

Even had their mouths not come together again, she wouldn't have said a word in protest, because the fire was too hot, the sweetness too sweet to deprive herself of this little bit of heaven. Web had always been this for her, a flame licking at her nerve ends, spreading a molten desire within her that water couldn't begin to quench.

He cupped her breast through the knit of her over-blouse, molding it to his palm, kneading and circling until at last his fingers homed in on the tight nub at its crest. Her flesh swelled, and she arched up, seeking even closer contact with the instrument of such bliss. She'd been starving for years; now she couldn't get enough. It was sheer relief when he impatiently tugged the overblouse from her hips.

"Lift up, sweet...there...I need...to touch you, Marni!"

She helped him, because she needed the very same thing, and she was tossing the blouse aside even as Web unhooked her bra and tore it away. Then he was lying half over her again, his large hand greedily rediscovering her blossoming flesh, and she was moaning in delight, straining for more, bunching the damp skin of his back in hands that clenched and unclenched, shifted, then clenched again.

She was in a frenzy. The tight knot in her belly was growing, inflamed not only by his thorough exploration of her nakedness but by the hardness of his sex pressing boldly against her thigh. When he slid down, she dug her fingers into his hair, holding on for dear life as his mouth opened over her breast, his tongue bathed it, his teeth closed around one distended nipple and tugged a path to her womb.

"Web!" she cried. "Oh, God, I need . . . I need . . ."

He slid back up, and her hand lowered instinctively to him, cupping him, caressing him until even that wasn't enough. His hand tangled with hers then, clutching at the tab of his zipper, tugging it down. He took her fingers and led them inside his briefs. He was trembling as badly as she was, and his voice shook with urgency.

"Touch me . . . touch me, sunshine . . ."

This time the pet name was so perfectly placed, so very right that it was stimulation in and of itself. She touched him, stroked him, pleasured him until he gave a hoarse cry of even greater need. Then he was tugging at her pants, freeing her hips for his invasion.

What happened then was something neither Marni nor Web had expected. She felt his tumescence press against the nest of curls at the apex of her thighs, and it was so intense, so electric that she recoiled and, in a burst of emotion, began to cry.

"Web...oh..." she sobbed, tears streaking down her cheeks and into the hairs of his chest. "Web...I...I..."

She couldn't say anything else. Her crying prevented it. He held her head tightly to his chest with his left arm and ran his good hand over and around her naked back, knowing that he could easily be inside her but ignoring that fact because, at the moment, her emotional state was far more important.

"It's okay. Shhhhh. Shhhhh."

"I want," she gulped, "want you...so badly, but...but..."

"Shhhhh. It's okay."

She wiped the tears from her eyes, but they kept flowing. She felt frustrated and embarrassed and confused. So she simply gave herself up to the outpouring of whatever it was and waited until at last the tears slowed before trying to speak again.

"I'm sorry...I didn't mean to do that...I don't know what happened..."

"Something's bothering you," he said softly, patiently. "Something snapped."

"But it's awful...what I did. A woman has no right to do that to...to a man."

"I know you want me, so you're suffering, too."

She raised wide, tear-filled eyes to his. "Let me help you." Her hand started back down. "Let me do it, Web—"

He flattened her body against his, trapping her hand. "No. I don't want that."

"But you'll be uncomfortable—"

"The discomfort is more in my mind than my body." Her tears had instantly cooled his ardor. He allowed a small space between them. "Feel. You'll see. Go on."

She did as he told her and discovered that he was no longer hard. Her eyes widened all the more, and she suddenly grappled with her pants, tugging them up. "You *don't* want me . . ."

He gave a short laugh and rolled his eyes to the ceiling. "I'm damned if I do and damned if I don't." His gaze fell to catch hers. "Of course I want you, sunshine. You are my sunshine, y'know. You're bright and warm, the source of an incredible energy, but only when you're sure of yourself, when you're happy. Something happened just now. I don't know exactly what it was, but it's pushed that physical drive into the background for the time being."

Marni wasn't sure what to think. She nervously matted the hair on his chest with the flat of her finger. "It used to be that nothing could push that physical drive into the background."

"We're older. Life is more complex than it used to be. When I was twenty-six, sex was a sheer necessity. It was a physical outlet, sure, but it was also a means of communicating things that either I didn't understand or didn't see or didn't want to say." His arm was beginning to throb. Shifting himself back against the pillow, he drew Marni against him, cradling her with his right arm, letting his left rest limply on the sheet.

"If I was still twenty-six, I'd have made love to you regardless of your tears just now. I wouldn't have had the strength to stop, the control. But I'm not twenty-six. I'm forty. I have the control now, and the strength." He paused for a minute, but there was more he wanted to say. "I haven't been a monk all these years, Marni. For a while I was with any and every woman who turned me on. Then I realized that the turn-on was purely physical, and it wasn't enough. Maybe I've mellowed. I've become picky. I think . . . I think that when we do make love, you and I, it'll be an incredibly new and wonderful experience."

To her horror, Marni began to cry again. "Why do you...do you *say* things like that, Web? Why are...are you so incredibly understanding?"

He hugged her tighter. "It hurts me when you cry, sunshine. Please, tell me what's bothering you. Tell me what happened back there."

"Oh, God," she cried, then sniffled, "I wish I knew. I was so high, so unbelievably high, and then it was like...like this door opened somewhere in the back of my mind, and in a lightning-quick instant I felt burned to a crisp, and frightened and nervous and guilty..."

He held her face back. "Guilty?"

She looked at him blankly, her lashes spiked with tears when she blinked. "Did I say that?" she whispered, puzzled.

"Very clearly. What did you mean?"

"I don't know. Maybe...maybe it's that we haven't been together long..."

"Maybe," he returned, but skeptically. "You've been with other men since that summer, haven't you?"

She nodded. "But it's been a long time for me and... maybe it was too easy and that bothered me."

"You've always been honest with me, Marni," he chided softly. "Tell me. These are modern times, and you're a fully grown, experienced woman. If you met a guy and felt something really unique with him, and if he felt the same, and the two of you wanted desperately to make love, would you hold out on principle?" When she didn't answer, he coaxed gently, "Would you?"

"No," she whispered.

"But you do feel guilty now. Why, sunshine? Why guilty?"

"Maybe it was too fast. And your hand..."

"My hand wasn't hurting just then. Loving you blotted everything out. I wasn't complaining, or moaning. Come on, Marni. Why guilty?"

Her gaze darted blindly about the room. She frowned, swallowed hard, then began to breathe raggedly. "I guess...I guess that...maybe I felt that...well, we'd made love so much during that summer, and it was so good and right, and then...and then..." Her eyes were wide when she raised them to his. Fresh tears pooled on her lower lids but refused to overflow. "And then the accident happened and Ethan was killed and you were in the hospital and my parents...forbade me to...see you..."

Web closed his eyes. An intense inner pain brought a soft moan to his lips, and he slipped both arms around her. "Lord, what they've done...what they've done..."

He held her for a long time without saying a word, because only then did he realize the enormity of the hurdle he faced.

5

WEB HAD MUCH to consider. He understood now that there was a link in Marni's mind between their lovemaking of fourteen years ago and Ethan's death. He understood that, though she may not have been aware of it at the time, some small part of her had felt guilty about their affair, and Ethan's death must have seemed to her a form of punishment. And he understood that her parents had done nothing to convince her it wasn't so.

Much to consider...so much to consider. He held Marni tightly, wanting desperately to protect her, to take away the pain. She was such a strong woman, yet still fragile. He tried to decide what to do, what to say. In the end he wasn't any more ready to discuss this newly revealed legacy of that summer in Maine than she was.

"Marni?" he murmured against her hair. He ran his hand soothingly over her naked back, then kissed her forehead. "Sweetheart?"

Marni, too, had been stunned by what she'd said. But rather than think of it, she'd closed her eyes and let the solid warmth of Web's body calm her. She took a last, faintly erratic breath. "Hmmm?"

"Are you any good at brewing coffee?"

She knew what he was doing and was grateful. A faint smile formed against his chest, and she opened her eyes. "Not bad."

"Think you could do it while I use the bathroom? I'm feeling a little muzzy right about now."

His voice did sound muzzy, so she took pity on him. Reaching for her discarded blouse, she dragged it over her breasts as she sat up. "I think I could handle that."

He was looking at the blouse, then at the hands that clutched it to her. "Hey, what's this?" he asked very softly, gently. When he met her gaze, his blue eyes were infinitely tender. "You never used to cover up with me."

Embarrassed, she looked away. "That was fourteen years ago," she whispered.

"And you don't think that what we have now is as close?"

"It isn't that . . ."

He lightly curled his fingers over her slender shoulders. "What is it, sunshine? Please, tell me."

Her eyes remained downcast. "I . . . I'm older . . . I look different now."

"But I saw you a few minutes ago. I touched you and tasted you, and you were beautiful."

"That was in the heat of passion."

"And you're afraid I'll look at you now and see a thirty-one-year-old body and not be turned on?"

She shrugged. "Time does things."

"To me, too. Don't you think I'm aware that my body is older? I'm forty, not twenty-six. Do you think I'm not that little bit nervous that you'll see all the changes?"

Her gaze shot to him. "But I saw you last night, and not in passion, and you're body's better than ever!"

"So is yours, Marni," he whispered. Very slowly he eased the knit fabric from her hands and drew it away. His eyes took on a special light as they gently caressed her bare curves. "Your skin is beautiful. Your breasts are perfect."

"They're not as high as they used to be."

"They're fuller, more womanly." He didn't touch her, but his heart was thumping as he captured her gaze. "If I wanted a seventeen-year-old now, I'd have one. But I don't want that, Marni. I want a mature woman. I want you." Very gently he pulled her forward and pressed a warm kiss to each of her breasts in turn. She sucked in a sharp breath, and her nipples puckered instantly. "And if you don't get out of here this minute, mature woman," he growled only half in jest, "I'm going to have you." He shot a disparaging glance at the front of his jeans, then a more sheepish one back at her.

"Oh, Web," Marni breathed. She threw herself forward and gave him a final hug. "You always know the right thing to say."

He wanted to say that he didn't, but the words wouldn't come out because he'd closed his eyes and was caught up enjoying the silken feel of her against him. Only when the pressure in his loins increased uncomfortably did he force a hoarse warning. "Marni . . . that coffee?"

"Right away," she whispered, jumping up and running for the door, then returning, cheeks ablaze, for her bra and blouse before dashing for the kitchen.

Not only did she brew a pot of rich coffee, but by the time Web joined her she'd scrambled eggs, toasted English muffins and sliced fresh oranges for their breakfast.

"So you can cook," he teased. He remembered her telling him, during those days in Camden, that Cook had allowed no interference in the kitchen.

Marni put milk in his coffee, just as he'd had it that night when they'd been at the restaurant, and set the mug beside him. Then she joined him at the island counter. "I may not be a threat to Julia Child, but I've learned something. Post-graduate work, if you will."

He sipped the strong brew and smiled in appreciation. "An A for coffee." He took a forkful of the eggs, chewed appreciatively, then smacked his lips together. "An A for scrambled eggs. Very moist and light."

She laughed. "Don't grade the muffins or the orange. I really can't take much credit for either."

"Still, you didn't burn the muffins."

"You have a good toaster."

"And the orange is sliced with precision."

"You have a sharp knife, and I have a tidy personality." Amused, she was watching him eat. "You'll choke if you don't slow down."

"I'm suddenly starved. You should be, too. We didn't get around to having dinner last night.

Marni ate half of her eggs, then offered the rest to Web, who devoured them and one of her muffins as though his last meal had been days ago. When he was done, he sat back and studied her. "What now?" he asked softly.

"You're still hungry?"

"What now . . . for us? Will you stay a while?"

She'd been debating that one the whole time she'd been making breakfast. "I . . . think I'd better head home. A lot has happened. Too quickly. I need a little time."

He nodded. More than anything he wished she'd stay, but he understood her need for time alone to think. He could only hope it would be to his benefit.

She began to clean up the kitchen. "Will you be okay . . . your hand, and all?"

"I'll be fine. . . . Marni, what say we try for that picture again on Tuesday? If you can manage it with your schedule, I can make all the other arrangements."

She finished rinsing the frying pan, then reached for the dish towel. "Do you really think you'll be up for it?"

"I've got another shoot set for Monday. It has to go on, no matter what. I'll be up for it.... But that's not the real question here." Not wanting to put undue pressure on her, he remained where he was at the island. "Are you willing to give it another try?"

Her head was bowed. "You really think it's the cover we need?"

"I do. But more than that, I *want* to do it. You have no idea how much it means to me to photograph you and put your face out there for the world to see. I'm proud of you, Marni. Some men might want to keep you all to themselves, and I do in a lot of respects, but I'm a photographer, and you happen to mean more to me than any other subject I've ever photographed. I want you to be on the premier cover of *Class* because I feel you belong there, and because I feel that I'm the only one who can see and capture on film the beauty you are, inside and out." When she simply stood with her back to him, saying nothing, he grew more beseechful. "I know that may sound arrogant, but it's the way I feel. Give me a chance, Marni. Don't deny me this one pleasure."

"It's not only your eyes that get to me, Brian Webster," she muttered under her breath, "it's your tone of voice. How can you prey on my *vulnerability* this way?"

He knew then that he'd won. Rising, he crossed to the sink and gave her waist a warm squeeze. "Because I know that it's right, Marni. It's right all the way."

MARNI STILL HAD her doubts. She left him soon after that and returned to her apartment. She had errands to run that afternoon—food shopping, a manicure, stockings to buy— and she would have put them all off in a minute if she'd felt it wise to stay longer with Web. But she did need to be alone, and she did need to think. At least, that was what she told herself. Then she did everything possible to avoid being alone, to avoid thinking.

She dallied in the supermarket, spent an extra hour talking with the woman whose manicure followed hers, and whom she'd come to know for that reason, then browsed through every department of Bloomingdale's before reaching the hosiery counter. When she finished her shopping, she returned home in time to put her purchases away, then shower and dress for the cocktail party she'd been invited to. It was a business-related affair, and when she got there she threw herself into it, so much so that when she finally got home she was exhausted and went right to bed.

When she woke up the next morning, though, Web was first and foremost on her mind. She thought back to the same hour the day before, remembering being on his bed, on the verge of making love with him. Her body throbbed at the memory. She took a long shower, but it didn't seem to help. Without considering the whys and wherefores, she picked up the phone and dialed his number.

"Webster, here," was the curt answer.

She hesitated, then ventured cautiously, "Web?"

He paused, then let out a smiling sigh. "Marni. How are you, sunshine?"

"I'm okay.... Am I disturbing you?"

"Not on your life."

"You sounded distracted."

"I was sitting here feeling sorry for myself. Just about to drag out the old morgue book."

"Why feeling sorry for yourself?"

"Because I'm here and you're there, and because my hand hurts and I'm wondering how in hell I'm going to manage tomorrow."

"It's still really bad?"

"Nah. It's a little sore, but self-pity always makes things seem worse."

She grinned. "Then, by all means, drag out the old morgue book."

"I won't have to, now that you've called.... I tried you last night."

She'd been wondering about that, worrying . . . hoping. "I had to go to a cocktail party. It was a business thing. Pretty dry." In hindsight that was exactly what it had been, though she'd convinced herself otherwise at the time. No, not really dry, but certainly not as exciting as it might have been had Web been there.

"I sat here alone all night thinking of you," he said without remorse.

"That's not fair."

"I'll say it's not. You're out there munching on scrumptious little hors d'oeuvres while I dig into the peanut butter jar—"

"It's not fair that you're making me feel guilty," she corrected him, but she was grinning. If he'd spent last night with a gorgeous model, she'd have been jealous as hell.

He feigned resignation with an exaggerated sigh. "No need to feel guilty. I'm used to peanut butter—"

"Web . . ." she warned teasingly.

"Okay. But I really did miss you. I do miss you. Yesterday at this time we were having breakfast together."

"I know." There was a wistfulness to her tone.

"Hey, I could pick you up in an hour and we could go for brunch."

"No, Web. I have work to do. I promised myself I'd stay in all day and get it done."

"Work? On the weekend?"

She knew he was mocking her, but she didn't mind. "I always bring a briefcase home with me. Things get so hectic at the office sometimes that I need quiet time to reread proposals and reports."

"I wouldn't keep you more than an hour, hour and a half at most."

"I . . . I'd better not."

"You still need time to think."

"Yes."

He spoke more softly. "That I can accept.... We're on for Tuesday, aren't we?"

"I'll have to work it out with my secretary when I go in tomorrow, but I don't think I have anything that can't be shifted around."

"I've already called Anne. She'll have Marjorie get some clothes ready, but I said that I wanted as few people there for the actual shoot as possible. That'll go for my staff, too, and you can leave Edgar and Steve behind at the office."

"I will. Thank you."

He paused, his tone lightening. "Can I call you tomorrow night, just to make sure you don't get cold feet and back out on me at the last minute?"

"I won't back out once all the arrangements are made."

"Can I call you anyway?"

She smiled softly. "I'd like that."

"Good." He hated to let her go. Her voice alone warmed him, not to mention the visual picture he'd formed of her auburn hair framing her face, her cheeks bright and pink, her lips soft, the tips of her breasts peaking through a nightgown, or a robe, or a blouse—it didn't matter which, the effect was the same. "Well," he began, then cleared his throat, "take care, Marni."

"I will." She hated to let him go. His voice alone thrilled her, not to mention the visual picture she'd formed of his dark hair brushing rakishly over his brow, his lean, shadowed cheeks, his firm lips, the raw musculature of his torso.

She took an unsteady breath. "Are you sure you can manage everything with your hand?" If he'd said that he was having trouble, she would have rushed to his aid in a minute.

He was tempted to say he was having trouble, but he'd never been one to lie. "I'm sure. . . . Bye-bye, sweetheart."

"Bye, Web."

MARNI WOULD INDEED HAVE TRIED to back out on the photo session had it not been for the arrangements that had been made. Through all of Sunday, while she tried to concentrate first on the Sunday *Times*, then on her work, she found herself thinking of her relationship with Web. She was no longer seventeen and in that limbo between high school, college and the real world. She was old enough to have serious thoughts about the future, and she knew that with each additional minute she spent with Web those thoughts would grow more and more serious.

Though she wasn't sure exactly what he wanted, she knew from what he'd said that he envisioned some kind of future relationship with her. But there were problems—actually just one, but it was awesome. Her family.

It was this that weighed heavily on her when she arrived at Web's studio Tuesday morning. As he'd promised, Web had called the evening before. He'd been gentle and encouraging, so that when she'd hung up the phone she'd felt surprisingly calm about posing again. Then her mother had called.

"Marni, darling, why didn't you tell me! I had no idea what had happened until Tanya called a little while ago!"

Icy fingers tripped up Marni's spine. What did her mother know? She hadn't sounded angry. . . . What could *Tanya* know . . . or was it Marni's own guilty conscience at work? "What is it, Mother? What are you talking about?"

"That little business you witnessed on Friday night. Evidently there was a tiny notice in the paper yesterday. I missed it completely, and if it hadn't been for Tanya—"

Marni was momentarily stunned. She hadn't expected any of that episode to reach the press, much less with her name printed . . . and, she assumed, Web's. She moistened her lips, unsure as to how much more her mother knew. All she could say was a slightly cryptic, "Tanya reads the paper?"

"Actually it was Sue Beacham—you know, Tanya's friend whose husband is a state senator? They say he's planning to run for Congress, and he'll probably make it. He has more connections than God. Of course, Jim Heuer had the connections and it didn't help. He didn't get Ed Donahue's support, so he lost most of the liberal vote. I guess you can never tell about those things."

Marni took a breath for patience. Her mother tended to run on at the mouth, particularly when it came to name-dropping. "What was it that Sue saw?"

"There was a little article about how you and that photographer were instrumental in interrupting a rape."

"It wasn't a rape," Marni countered very quietly. "It was a mugging."

"But it could have been a rape if you hadn't come along, at least that was what the paper said. I'd already thrown it out, but Tanya had the article and read it to me."

Marni forced herself to relax. It appeared that Adele Lange hadn't made the connection between Brian Webster, the photographer, and the notorious Web. "It was really nothing, Mother. We happened to be walking down the street and heard the woman's cries. By the time we got to her, her assailant was already on his way."

"But this photographer you were with—it said he was injured."

"Just his hand. He's fine."

"Who is he, Marni? You never mentioned you were seeing a photographer, and such a renowned one, at least that's what Tanya says. She says that he's right up there with the best, and I'm sure I've seen his work but I've probably repressed the name. Webster." Her voice hardened. "I don't even like to say it."

Marni's momentary reprieve was snatched away. It didn't matter that her mother hadn't actually connected the two. What mattered was that the ill will lingered.

"Are you seeing him regularly?" Adele asked when Marni remained quiet.

"He's doing the cover work for the new magazine. There were some things we had to work out."

"Do you think you *will* be seeing him? Socially, that is? A photographer." Marni could picture her mother pursing her lips. "I think you should remember that a man in a field like his is involved with many, many women, and glamorous ones at that. You'll have to be careful."

The "many, many women" Marni's mother mentioned went along with the stereotype. Marni felt no threat on that score. Indeed, it was the least of her worries.

"Mother," she sighed, "you're getting a little ahead of yourself."

"It doesn't hurt to go into things with both eyes open."

"I've *got* both eyes open."

"All right, all right, darling. You needn't get riled up. I only called because I was concerned. I know incidents like that aren't uncommon, but witnessing it on the street can be a traumatic experience for a woman."

"It was traumatic for the victim. I'm okay."

"Are you sure? You sound tired."

"After a full day at the office, I am tired."

"Well, I guess you have a right to that. I'll let you rest, darling. Talk with you soon?"

"Uh-huh." Marni had hung up then, but she'd spent a good part of the night brooding, so she was tired and unsettled when Web came to greet her at the reception area of the studio. His smile was warm and pleasure-filled, relaxing her somewhat, but he was quick to see that something was amiss.

"Nervous?" he asked her as he guided her into the studio.

"A little."

"It'll be easier this time."

"I hope so."

"Is . . . everything all right?"

"Everything's fine."

"Why won't you look at me?"

She did then. "Better?"

He shook his head. "Smile for me."

She did then. "Better?"

He gestured noncommittally, but she was looking beyond him again, so he didn't speak. "See? It's almost quiet here."

Indeed it was. Anne, who appeared to be the only one present from *Class*, waved to her from the other side of the room, where she was in conference with the makeup artist. Marni recognized the hairstylist and, more vaguely, several of Web's assistants.

"Lee?" Web called out. A man turned from the group and, smiling, approached. "Lee, I'd like you to meet Marni. Formally. Marni, my brother, Lee."

Marni's smile was more genuine as she shook Lee's warm hand. He was pleasant-looking, though nowhere near as handsome or tall as Web. Wearing a suit, minus its tie, he was more conservatively dressed than the other men in the room, but his easy way made up for the difference. Marni liked him instantly.

"I'm pleased to meet you, Lee. Web's had only good things to say about you."

Lee shot Web a conspiratorial glance. "I'd have to say the same about you. I've heard about nothing else for the past week." He held up his hand. "Not that he's telling everyone, mind you, but—" he winked "—I think the old man needs an outlet."

Marni wondered just how much Lee knew, then realized that it didn't matter. He was Web's brother. The physical resemblance may have been negligible, but there was something deeper, an intangible quality the two men shared. She knew she'd trust Lee every bit as much as she trusted Web. Of course, trust wasn't really the problem....

"Enough," Web was saying with a smile. "We'd better get things rolling here."

Marni barely had time to squeeze Lee's arm before Web was steering her off toward the changing rooms. Once again she was "done over," this time more aware of what was happening. She asked questions—how the hairstylist managed such a smooth sweep from her crown, what the make-up artist had done for her eyes to make them seem so far apart—but she was simply making conversation, perhaps in her way apologizing for having spoiled these people's efforts the week before. And diverting her mind from the worry that set in each time she looked at Web.

If the villain of the previous Tuesday had been the shock and pain of memory, now it was guilt. Marni saw Web's face, so open and encouraging, then the horror-filled ones of her parents when they learned she was seeing him again. She heard his voice, so gentle in instruction, then the harsh, bitter words of her family when they knew she was associating with the enemy.

Web tried different poses from the week before, used softer background music. He tried different lights and different cameras—the latter mostly on his tripod, which he could more easily manage, but in the end holding the camera in his hand with his splinted pinkie sticking straight out.

Halfway through the session, he called a break, shooing everyone else away after Marni had been given a cool drink.

"What do you think?" she asked hesitantly. The face she made suggested that she had doubts of her own but needed the reassurance. "Any better than last week?"

"Better than that, but still not what I want. It's a little matter of . . . this . . . spot." With his forefinger, he lightly stroked the soft skin between her brows. "No amount of makeup is going to hide the creases when you frown."

"But I thought I was smiling, or doing whatever it was you asked me to do."

"You were. But those little creases creep in there anyway. When I ask for a tiny smile, the overall effect is one of pleading. When I ask for a broad smile, you look like you're in pain. When I ask you to wet your lips and leave them parted, you look like you're holding your breath."

"I am," she argued, throwing up a hand in frustration. "I'm no good at this. I told you, Web. This isn't my thing."

She was leaning against the arm of a director's chair. He stood close by, looking down at her. "It can't be the crowd, because there's no crowd today. It can't be the music, or the posing. And it can't be shock. Not anymore. . . . You're worried about something. That's what the creases tell me."

"I'm worried that I'll never be able to give you what you want, that you won't get your picture and you'll be disappointed and angry."

"Angry? Never. Disappointed? Definitely. But I'm not giving up yet. I'm going to get this picture, Marni. One way or another, I'm going to get it."

He spoke with such conviction, and went back to work with such determination, that Marni began to suspect he'd have her at it every day for a month, if that's what it took. She did her best to concentrate on relaxing her facial muscles, but found it nearly impossible. She'd get rid of the creases, but then her mouth would be wrong, or the angle of her head, or her shoulders.

The session ended not in a burst of tears as it had last time, but in sighs of fatigue from both her and Web. "Okay," he said resignedly as he handed his camera to one of his assistants, "we'll take a look at what we've got. There may be something." He ran his fingers through his hair. "God only knows I've exposed enough film."

Marni whirled around and stalked off toward the dressing room.

"Marni!" he called out, but she didn't stop. So he loped after her, enclosing them in the privacy of the small room. "What was that about? You walked out of there like I'd insulted you."

"You did." She removed the chunky beads from around her neck and put them on a nearby table. Two oversized bracelets soon followed. "You're disgusted with me. You never have to go through this with normal models. 'God only knows I've exposed enough film.' Did you have to say that, in that tone, for everyone in the room to hear?"

"It was a simple comment."

"It was an indictment."

"Then it was as much an indictment of me as it was of you. I'm the photographer! Half of my supposed skill is in drawing the mood and the look from a model!"

She was swiftly unbuttoning her blouse, heedless of Web's presence. "I'm the model. A rank amateur. You're the renowned photographer. If anyone's at fault, we both know who it is."

"Then you're angry at yourself, but don't lay that trip on me!"

"See? You agree!" She'd thrown the blouse aside and was fumbling with the waistband of her skirt. Her voice shook as she released the button and tugged down the zipper. "Well, I'm sorry if I've upset your normal pattern of success, but don't say I didn't warn you. Right from the beginning I knew this was a mad scheme. You need a *model*, an *experienced* model." She stumbled out of the skirt, threw it on top of the blouse, then grabbed for her own clothes and began to pull them on. "I can't be what you want, Web, no matter how much you want to think otherwise. I am what I am. I do what I do, and I do it well, and if there's baggage I carry—like little creases between my eyes—I can't help it." She'd stepped into her wool dress, but left it unbuttoned. Suddenly drained from her outburst, she lifted a hand to rub at those creases.

Web remained quiet. He'd reached the end of his own spurt of temper minutes ago and was simply waiting for her to calm down enough to listen to what he had to say. When she sighed and slumped into a nearby chair, he slowly approached and squatted beside her.

"Firstly, I'm not angry at you. If anything I'm angry at me, because there's something I'm missing and I don't know how to get at it. Secondly, I'm not really angry, just tired." He flexed his unbound fingers. "My left hand is stiff because I'm not used to working this way." He put his hand down on her knee. "Thirdly, and most importantly, it *is* you I want. I'm not looking for something you're not. I'm not trying to make you into someone else. You're such a unique and wonderful person Marni—it's *that* that I'm trying to capture on film.... Look at me," he said softly, drawing her hand from her face. "You're right. It is much easier photographing a 'normal model,' but only because there isn't half the depth, because

I can put there what I want. Creating a mood, a look, is one thing. Bringing out feeling, *individual* feeling is another. Don't you see? That's what's going to make this issue of *Class* stand out on the shelves. Not only are you beautiful to look at, but you'll have all those other qualities shining out from you. The potential reader of *Class* will say to herself, 'Hmmm, this looks interesting.'"

Marni was eyeing him steadily. Her expression had softened, taking on a glimmer of helplessness. He brushed the backs of his fingers against her cheek, thinking how badly he wanted to reach her, to soothe her.

"But what happened this morning," he went on in a whisper-soft tone, "what we've been arguing about in here is really secondary. You've got something on your mind that you haven't been able to shake. Share it with me, Marni. If nothing more, talking about it will make you feel better. Maybe I can help."

She only wished it were so. How could she say that she was falling in love with him again, but that her parents would never accept it? That they hated him, that she'd spent the last fourteen years of her life trying to make up for Ethan's death by being what he might have been if he'd lived, and that she didn't know if she had the strength to shatter her parents' illusion?

"Oh, Web," she sighed, slipping her arms over his shoulders and leaning forward to rest her check against his. "Life is so complicated."

He stroked her hair. "It doesn't have to be."

"But it is. Sometimes I wish I could turn the clock back to when I was seventeen and stop it there. Ethan would be alive, and you and I would be carrying on without a care in the world."

"We had cares. There was the problem of where to go so that we could be alone to love each other. And there was the problem of your parents, and what would happen if they found out about us."

Marni's arms tightened around him, and she rubbed her cheek against his jaw, welcoming the faint roughness that branded him man and so very different from her. She loved the smell of him, the feel of him. If only she could blot out the rest of the world . . .

"It's still a problem, isn't it, Marni?" She went very still, so he continued in the same gentle tone. "I'm no psychologist, but I've spent a lot of time thinking the past week, especially the past few days, about us and the future. Your parents despised me for what I was, and wasn't, and for what I'd done. They'd be a definite roadblock for us, wouldn't they?"

Just then a knock sounded at the door. Web twisted around and snapped, "Yes?"

The door opened, and a slightly timid Anne peered in. Uncomfortably, she looked from Web to Marni. "I'm sorry. I didn't mean to interrupt. I just wanted to know if there was anything I could do to help."

"No. Not just now," Marni said. "You can go back to the office. I'll be along later."

"I'll take a look at the contact sheets as soon as possible and let you know what I think," Web added quietly.

Anne nodded, then shut the door, at which point Web turned back to Marni.

She was gnawing on her lower lip. "Did you know that there was an article in the newspaper about the incident last Friday night?" she asked.

His jaw hardened. "Oh, yes. I got several calls from friends congratulating me on my heroism. Of all the things I'd like to be congratulated on, that isn't one. I could kick myself for not instructing the cops to leave our names off any report they might hand to the press. Neither of us needs that kind of publicity." He frowned. "You didn't mention the article when I spoke with you last night."

"I didn't know about it."

"Then . . . ?"

"My mother called right after you did."

He blinked slowly, lifted his chin, then lowered it. He might have been saying, "Ahhhhhh, that explains it."

"If you can believe it, my sister Tanya brought it to her attention." Marni's voice took on a mildly hysterical note. "Neither of them made the connection, Web. Neither one of them associated Brian Webster, the photographer, with you."

"But you thought at first they might have," he surmised gently, "and it scared the living daylights out of you."

Apologetically Marni nodded, then slid forward in the chair and buried her face against his throat. Her thighs braced his waist, but there was nothing remotely sexual about the pose. "Hold me, Web. Just hold me . . . please?"

She sighed when he folded his arms around her, knowing in that instant that this would be all she needed in life if only the rest of humanity could fade away.

"Do you love me, Marni?" he asked hoarsely.

"I think I do," she whispered in dismay.

"And I love you. Don't you think that's a start?"

She raised her head. "You love me?"

"Uh-huh."

"When did you . . . You didn't before . . ."

He knew she was referring to that summer in Maine. "No, I didn't before. I was too young. You were too young. I didn't know where I was going, and the concept of love was beyond me."

"But when . . . ?"

"Last weekend. After you left me, I realized that I didn't want anyone but you pushing aspirin down my throat."

She pinched his ribs, but she wasn't smiling. "Don't tease me."

"I'm not. No one's ever taken care of me before. I've always wanted to be strong and in command. But somehow being myself with you, being able to say that I'm tired or that I hurt, seemed right. Not that I want to do it all the time—I'm not a hypochondriac. But I want to be able to take care of you like you did me. TLC, and for the first time, the L means something."

Marni lowered her head and pressed closer to him, feeling the strong beat of his heart as though it and her own were all that existed. "I do love you, Web. The second time around it feels even stronger. If only... if only we could forget about everything else."

"We can."

"It's not possible."

"It is, for a little while, if we want."

She raised questioning eyes to his urgent ones.

"Come to Vermont with me this weekend. Just the two of us, alone and uninterrupted. We can talk everything out then and decide what to do, but most importantly we can be with each other. I think we need it. I think we deserve it.... What do you say?"

She sighed, feeling simultaneously hopeless and incredibly light-headed. "I say that it's crazy.... The whole thing's crazy, because the problems aren't going to go away... but how can I refuse?" A slow grin spread over her face, soon matched by his. He hugged her again, then kissed her. It was a sweet kiss, deep in emotion rather than physicality. When it ended, she clung to him for a long time. "I feel a little like I'm seventeen again and we've just arranged an illicit rendezvous. There's something exciting about stealing away, knowing my parents would be furious if they knew, but doing it all the same."

He took her face in his hands and spoke seriously. "We're adults now. Independent, consenting adults. In the end, it doesn't matter what your parents think, Marni."

Theoretically speaking, he was right, she knew. Idealistically she couldn't have agreed with him more. Practically speaking, though, it was a dream. But then, Web hadn't grown up in her house, with her parents. He hadn't gone into her family's business. He hadn't been in her shoes when Ethan had died, and he wasn't in her shoes now. "Later," she whispered. "We'll discuss it later. Right now, let's just be happy..."

MARNI WAS HAPPY. She blocked out all thoughts except one—that she loved Web and he loved her. And she was *very* happy. Business took her to Richmond on Wednesday morning, but she called Web that night, and he was at the airport to meet her when she returned on Thursday evening. Her suitcase had been emptied and repacked, and was waiting by her door when he came to pick her up late Friday afternoon.

"I hope you know I've shocked everyone at the office," she quipped, shrugging into her down jacket. "They've never known me to leave work so early."

He arched a brow. "Did you tell them where you were going?"

"Are you kidding? And spoil the sense of intrigue?"

Web was more practical. It wasn't that he wanted any interruptions during the weekend, but neither did he want the police out searching for her. "What if there's an emergency? What if someone needs to reach you and can't? Shouldn't you leave my number with someone?"

"Actually, I did. Just the number. With my administrative assistant. If anyone wants me that badly, they'll know to contact her. She'll be able to tell from the area code that I'm in Vermont, but that's about it."

Web was satisfied. He felt no fondness for her parents, but regardless of her age, they might worry if she seemed to have disappeared from the face of the earth. He knew that *he*'d be sick with worry if he tried to reach her and no one knew where she was.

"Good girl," was all he said before grabbing her suitcase and leading her to the waiting car.

The drive north was progressively relaxing. The tension of the day-to-day world, embodied by the congestion of traffic, thinned out and faded. Marni's excitement grew. Her eyes brightened, her cheeks took on a natural rosy glow. She had only to look to her left and see Web for her heart to feel lighter and lighter until she felt she was floating as weightlessly as those few snowflakes that drifted through the cold Vermont night air.

Web suggested that they stop for supplies at the village market near his house, so that they wouldn't have to go out again if the weather got bad. Marni was in full agreement.

"So where is your place?" she asked when they'd left the market behind. "I see houses and lots of condominium complexes—"

"They're sprouting up everywhere. Vacation resort areas, they're called. You buy your own place, then get the use of a central facility that usually includes a clubhouse, a restaurant or two, a pool, sometimes a lake or even a small ski slope. Not exactly my style, and I'm not thrilled with all the development. Pretty soon the place will be overrun with people. Fortunately where I am is off the beaten track."

"Where *are* you?"

He grinned and squeezed her knee. "Coming soon, sunshine. Be patient. Coming soon."

Not long after, he turned off the main road onto a smaller dirt one. The car jogged along, climbing steadily until at last they reached a clearing.

Marni caught her breath. "It's a log cabin," she cried in delight. "And you're on your own mountain!"

"Not completely on my own, but the nearest neighbor is a good twenty-minute trek through the trees." He pulled into the shelter of an oversized carport on the far side of the house.

"This is great! What a change from the city!"

"That's why I like it." He turned off the engine and opened his door. "Come on. It'll be cold inside, but the heat'll come up pretty quickly."

"Heat? That *has* to be from an old Franklin stove."

He chuckled. "I'm afraid I'm more pampered than that. It's baseboard heating. But I do have a huge stone fireplace . . . if that makes you feel better."

"Oh, yes," she breathed, then quickly climbed from the car and tugged her coat around her. The air was dry, with a sharp nip to it. Snow continued to fall, but it was light, enchanting rather than threatening. Marni wondered if anything could threaten her at that moment. She felt bold and excited and happy.

She looked at Web and beamed. She was in love, and in this place, so far from the city, she felt free.

6

TO MARNI'S AMAZEMENT, what had appeared to be a log cabin was, from within, like no log cabin she'd ever imagined. Soon after Web had bought the place, he'd had it gutted and enlarged. Rich barnboard from ceiling to floor sealed in the insulation he'd added. The furniture was likewise of barnboard, but plushly cushioned in shades of hunter green and cocoa. Though there was a hall leading to the addition that housed Web's bedroom and a small den, all Marni saw at first was the large living area, with the kitchen and dining area at its far end. Oh, yes, there was a huge stone fireplace. But rather than being set into a wall as she'd pictured, it was a three-hundred-and-sixty-degree one with steel supports that would cast its warm glow over the entire room.

Like the apartment above Web's studio, there was a sparseness to the decor, a cleanness of line, though it was very clearly country rather than city, and decidedly cozy.

After Marni had admired everything with unbounded enthusiasm, she helped Web stow the food they'd bought. Then he opened a bottle of wine, poured them each a glass and led her to the living area, where he set to work building a fire. The kindling caught and burned, and the dried logs were beginning to flame when he came to sit beside her on the sofa, opening an arm in an invitation she accepted instantly.

"I'm so happy I'm here with you," she whispered, rubbing her cheek against the wool of his sweater as she snuggled close to him.

He tightened his arm and pressed a slow kiss to her forehead. "So am I. This has always been my private refuge. Now it's *our* private refuge, and nothing could seem righter."

She tipped her head back. "Righter? Is that a word?"

"It is now," he murmured, then lowered his head and took her lips in a slow, deep, savoring kiss that left Marni reeling. Dizzily she set her wine on the floor and shifted, with Web's eager help, onto his lap, coiling her arms around his neck, closing her eyes in delight as she brushed her cheek against his jaw.

"I love you," she whispered, "love you so much, Web."

He set his own wine down and framed her face with his hands. His mouth breezed over each of her features before renewing acquaintance with her mouth. A deep, moist kiss, a shift in the angle of his head, a second deep, moist kiss. The exchange of breath in pleasured sighs. The evocative play of tongues, tips touching, circling, sliding along each other's length.

Marni hadn't had more than a sip of her wine, but she was high on love, high on freedom. She was breathing shallowly, with her head resting on his shoulder, when he began to caress her. She held her breath, concentrating on the intensity of sensation radiating from his touch. He spread his large hands around her waist, moved them up over her ribs and around to her back in slow, sensitizing strokes.

"I love you, sunshine," he whispered hoarsely, deeply affected by her sweet scent, her softness and warmth, her pliance, her emotional commitment. He brought his hands forward and inched them upward, covering her breasts, kneading them gently as she sighed against his neck.

Everything was in slow motion, unreal but exquisitely real. He caressed her breasts while she stroked the hair at his nape. He stroked her nipples while she caressed his back. They kissed again, and it was an exchange of silent vows, so deep and heartfelt that Marni nearly cried at its beauty.

"I was going to give you time," Web whispered roughly. His body was taut with a need he couldn't have hidden if he tried. "I was going to give you time . . . I hadn't intended an instant seduction."

"Neither had I," she breathed no less roughly. Her eyes held the urgency transmitted by the rest of her body. "I'm so pleased just to be here with you...but I want you...want to make love to you."

As much as her words inflamed him, he couldn't forget the last time they'd tried. "Are you sure? No doubts? Or guilt?"

She was shaking her head, very sure. "Not here. Not now." She pulled at his sweater. "Take this off. I want to touch you."

He whipped the sweater over his head, and she started working at the buttons of his shirt. When they were released, she spread the fabric wide, gave a soft sigh of relief and splayed her fingers over his hair-covered chest.

"You're so beautiful," she whispered in awe. Her hands moved slowly, exploring the sinewed swells of him, delving to the tight muscles of his middle before rising again and seeking the flat nipples nested amid whirls of soft, dark hair. She rubbed their tips until they stood hard, and didn't take her eyes from her work until Web forced her head up and hungrily captured her mouth.

His kiss left her breathless, and forehead to forehead they panted until at length he reached for the hem of her sweater and slowly drew it up and over her head. Slowly, too, he released one button, then the next, and in an instant's clear thought Marni reflected on the leisure of their approach. Fourteen years ago, when they'd come together for the first time, it had been in a fevered rush of arms and legs and bodies. Last Saturday the fever had been similar, as though they'd had to consummate their union before either of them had had time to think.

This time was different. They were in love. They were alone, in the cocoon of a cabin whose solid walls, whose surrounding forest warded off any and every enemy. This time there was a beauty in discovering and appreciating every inch of skin, every swell, every sensual conduit. This time it was heaven from the start.

Entranced, Marni watched as Web pushed her blouse aside. He unhooked her bra and gently peeled it from her breasts, then with a soft moan he very slowly traced her fullness, with first his fingertips, then the flat of his fingers, then his palm. She was swelling helplessly toward him, biting her lip to keep from crying out, when he finally took the full weight of her swollen flesh and molded his hands to it. His thumbs brushed over her nipples. Already taut, they puckered all the more, and she had to press her thighs together to still what was too quickly becoming a raging inferno.

Web didn't miss the movement. "Here . . ." He raised her for an instant, brought her leg around so that she straddled him, and settled her snugly against his crotch. With that momentary comfort, he returned his attention to her breasts.

"Web . . . Web . . ." she breathed. Her arms were looped loosely around his neck, her forehead hot against his shoulder. He was stroking her nipples again, and the action sent live currents through her body to her womb. Helplessly, reflexively, she began to slowly undulate her hips. "What you do to me—it's so . . . powerful. . . ."

"It's what I feel for you, what you feel for me that makes it so good."

She was shaking her head in amazement. "I used to think it was good back then . . . because we do have this instant attraction . . . but I can't *believe* what . . . I'm feeling now."

"Then feel, sunshine." He slipped his hands to her shoulders and pushed her blouse completely off, then her bra. "I want you to feel this. . ." He cupped her breasts and brought them to his chest, rubbing nipple to nipple until she wasn't the only one to moan. "And this . . ." He sought her lips and kissed her hotly, while his fingers found the snap of her jeans, lowered the zipper and slid inside.

He was touching her then, opening her, stroking deeper and deeper until she was moving against his hand, taking tiny, gasping breaths, instinctively stretching her thighs apart in a need for more.

Her control was slipping, but she didn't want it to. She wanted the beauty to last forever, no, longer. Putting a shaky hand around Web's wrist, she begged him, "Please . . . I want to touch you, too . . . I need to . . ."

"But I want you to come," he said in a hushed whisper by her ear.

"This way, later. The first time—now—I want you inside. Please . . . take off your pants, Web . . ."

His fingers stopped their sweet torment and slowly, reluctantly, withdrew. He didn't move to take off his clothes until he'd kissed her so thoroughly that she thought she'd disintegrate there and then. But she didn't, and he shifted her from his lap, sat forward to rid himself of his shirt, then stood and peeled off the rest of his clothes. For a moment, just before lowering his jeans, he suddenly wished he hadn't been as adept at building that fire and that it was still pitch-black in the room. The last thing he wanted was to spoil the mood by having Marni see his scars. But they were there; he couldn't erase them, and if she loved him . . .

Marni sat watching, enthralled as more and more of his flesh was revealed. It was a long minute before she even saw his leg, so fascinated had she been with what else was now bare. But inevitably her gaze fastened on the multiple lines, some jagged, others straight, that formed a frightening pattern along the length of his right thigh.

"Web?" She caught her breath and, eyes filling with tears, looked up at him. "You didn't tell me . . . I didn't know. . . ."

Quickly he knelt by her side and took both of her hands tightly in his. "Forget them, sweetheart. They're part of the past, and the past has no place here and now."

"But so many—"

"And all healed. No pain. No limp. Forget them. They don't matter." When she remained doubtful, he began to whisper kisses over her face. "Forget them," he breathed against her eyelids, then her lips. "Just love me . . . I need that more than anything . . ."

More than anything, that was what Marni needed, too. So she forgot. She pushed all thought of his scars and what had caused them from her mind. He was right. The past had no place here and now, and she refused to let it infringe on her present happiness. There would be a time to discuss scars she assured herself dazedly, but that time wasn't now, when the tender kisses he was raining over her face and throat, when the intimate sweep of his hands on her breasts was making clear thought an impossibility.

Her already simmering blood began to boil when he stood and reached for her hands to draw her up. She resisted, instead flattening her palms on his abdomen, moving them around and down. Gently, wonderingly, she encircled him and began a rhythmic stroking.

If he'd had any qualms about her reaction to his forty-year-old body, or fears that the sight of his leg would dull her desire, they were put soundly to rest by her worshipful ministration. He was digging his fingers into her shoulders by the time she leaned and pressed soft, wet kisses to his navel. Her hands, holding him, were between her breasts. Tucking in her chin, she slid her lips lower.

He was suddenly forcing her chin up, a pained smile on his face. "You don't play fair," he managed tightly. "I'm not made of stone."

"But I want you to—"

"This way, later," he whispered, repeating her earlier words. "For now, though, you were right . . ." When he reached for her hands this time, she stood, then with his help took off the rest of her clothes. They looked at each other, drenched in the pale orange glow of the fire. Then they came together, bare bodies touching for the first time in fourteen years, and it was so strangely new yet familiar, so stunningly electric yet right, that once again tears filled Marni's eyes and this time trickled down her cheeks.

Web felt them against his chest, and his arms tightened convulsively around her. "Oh, no . . ."

"Just joy, Web," she said as she laughed, then sniffled. "Tears of joy." She had her arms wrapped around his neck and held on while he lowered them both to the woven rug before the fire. Bracing himself on his elbows, he traced the curve of her lips with the tip of his tongue. She tried to capture him, but he eluded her, so she raised her head and tried again. Soon he was thrusting his tongue into her welcoming mouth, thrusting and retreating only to thrust again when she whimpered in protest at the momentary loss.

She welcomed the feel of his large body over hers. She felt sheltered, protected, increasingly aroused by everything masculine about him. Her hands skated over the corded swells of his back, glided to his waist and spread over his firm buttocks. She arched up to the hand he'd slipped between their bodies and offered him her breasts, her belly, the smoldering spot between her legs.

They touched and caressed, whispered soft words of love, of pleasure, of urging as their mutual need grew. It was as if nothing in the world could touch them but each other, as if that touch was life-giving and life-sustaining to the extent that their beings were defined by it. Web's lips gave form and substance to each of Marni's features, as his hands did to her every feminine curve. Her mouth gave shape and purpose to his, as her hands did to his every masculine line.

Finally, locked in each other's gaze, they merged fully. Web filled her last empty place, bowed his back and pressed even more deeply until he touched the entrance to her womb.

"I love you," he mouthed, unable to produce further sound.

The best she could do was to brokenly mouth the words back. Her breath seemed caught in her throat, trapped by the intensity of the moment. She'd never felt as much of a person, as much of a woman as she did now, with Web's masculinity surrounding her, filling her, completing her. Fourteen years ago they'd made love, and it had been breathtaking, too, but so different. Now she was old enough to understand and appreciate the full value of what she and Web shared. The extraordinary pleasure was emotional as well as physical, a total commitment on both of their parts to that precious quality of togetherness.

Web felt it, too. As he held himself still, buried deep inside Marni, he knew that he'd never before felt the same pleasure, the same satisfaction with another woman. The pleasure, the satisfaction, encompassed not only his body but his mind and heart as well, and the look of wonder on Marni's face told him the feeling was shared.

Slowly he began to move, all the while watching her. Waves of bliss flowed over her features as he thrust gently, then with increasing speed and force as she moved in tempo beneath him. The act he'd carried through so many times before seemed to have taken on an entirely new and incredible intimacy that added fuel to the flame in his combustive body.

Harder and deeper he plunged, his ardor matched by her increasing abandon. Before long they were both lost in a world of glorious sensation, a world that grew suddenly brilliant, then blinding. Marni caught her breath, arched up and was suspended for a long moment before shattering into paroxysms of mindless delight. The air left her lungs in choked spurts, but she was beyond noticing, as was Web, whose own body tensed, then jerked, then shuddered.

Only when the spasms had ended and his limbs grew suddenly weak did he collapse over her with a drawn-out moan. "Marni . . . my God! I've never . . . *never* . . ." He buried his face in the damp tendrils of hair at her neck and whispered, "I love you . . . so much . . ."

Marni was as limp and weak, but nothing could have kept the broad smile from her face. Words seemed inadequate, so she simply draped her arms over his shoulders, closed her eyes . . . and smiled on.

It was some time later before either of them moved, and then it was Web, sliding to her side, bringing her along to face him. He brushed the wayward fall of hair from her cheeks and let his hand lightly caress her earlobe.

"You give so much, so much," he whispered. "I almost feel as though I don't deserve it."

She pressed her fingers to his lips, then stroked them gently. "I could say the same to you."

He smiled crookedly. "So why don't you?"

"Because you know how I feel."

"Tell me anyway. My ego needs boosting, since the rest of me is totally deflated."

She grinned, but the grin mellowed into a tender smile as she spoke. "You're warm and compassionate, incredibly intelligent and sensitive. And you're sexy as hell."

"Not right now."

"Yes, right now." She raked the hair from his brow and let her fingers tangle in its thickness. "Naked and sweaty and positively gorgeous, you'd bring out the animal in me—" she gave a rueful chuckle "—if I had the strength."

"S'okay," he murmured, rolling to his back and drawing her against him, "a soft, purring kitten is all I can handle right about now. You exhaust me, sunshine, inside and out."

"The feeling's mutual, Brian Webster," she sighed, but it was a happy sigh, in keeping with the moment.

They lay quietly for a time, listening to the beat of each other's heart, the lazy cadence of their breathing, the crackling of the fire behind them.

"It's funny, hearing you call me that," he mused, rubbing his chin against her hair. "Brian. It sounds so formal."

"Not formal, just...strange. I keep trying to picture your mother calling you that when you were a little boy. 'Brian! Come in the house this minute, Brian!' When did they start calling you Web?"

"My mother never did, or my stepfather, for that matter. But the kids in school—you know how kids are, trying to act tough calling each other by their last names, then when they're a little older finding nicknames that fit. Web just seemed to fit. By the time I'd graduated from high school, I really thought of myself as Web."

"Did you consciously decide to revert to Brian when you got into photography?"

"It was more a practical thing at that point. I had to sign my name to legal forms—model releases, magazine contracts, that kind of thing. People started calling me Brian." He gave a one-shouldered shrug. "So Brian I became. Again."

"We'll call our son Brian."

He jerked his head up and stared at her. "Our son?"

She put her fingers back on his lips. "Shhh. Don't say another word. This is a dream weekend, and I'm going to say whatever I feel like saying without even thinking of 'why' or 'if' or 'how.' I intend to give due consideration to every impulse that crosses my mind, and the impulse on my mind at this particular moment is what we'll name our son. Brian. I do like it."

Once over the initial shock of Marni's blithe reference to "our son," Web found that he liked her impulsiveness. He grinned. "You're a nut. Has anyone ever told you that?"

"No. No one. I'm not usually prone to nuttiness. You do something to my mind, Web. Or maybe log cabins do something to me. Or mountains."

He propped himself on an elbow and smiled down at her. "Tell me more. What other impulses would you like to give due consideration to?"

"Dinner. I'm starved. Maybe *that*'s why I'm momentarily prone to nuttiness. I didn't eat lunch so I could leave the office that much earlier, and I can't remember breakfast, it was that long ago. I think I'm running on fumes."

Web nuzzled her neck. "I love these fumes. Mmmm, do I love these fumes."

Light-headed and laughing, Marni clung to him until, with a final nip at her neck, he hauled himself to his feet and gave her a hand up. He cleared his throat. "Dinner. I think I could use it, too." He ran his eyes the length of her flushed and slender body. "Did you bring a robe?"

"Uh-huh."

"Think you could get it?"

"Uh-huh."

". . . Well?"

She hadn't moved. Her eyes were on his leanly muscled frame. "Have *you* got one?"

"Uh-huh."

"Think you could get it?"

"Uh-huh."

". . . Well?"

Their gazes met then, and they both began to smile. If they'd been back in New York, they'd probably have made love again there and then, lest they lose the opportunity. But they were in Vermont, with the luxury of an entire weekend before them. There was something to be said for patience, and anticipation.

With a decidedly male growl, Web dragged her to his side and started off toward the bedroom, where he'd left their bags. Moments later, dressed in terry velour robes that were coincidentally similar in every respect but color—Web's was wine, Marni's white—they set to the very pleasant task of making dinner together. When Web opted out of chores such as slicing tomatoes and mushrooms for a salad, claiming that he was hampered by his injured hand, Marni mischievously remarked that his injured hand hadn't hampered his amorous endeavors. When Marni opted out of putting a match to the pilot light of the stove, claiming that she didn't like to play with fire, Web simply arched a devilish brow in silent contradiction.

They ate by the fire, finishing the wine they'd barely sipped earlier. Then, leaving their dishes on the floor nearby, they made sweet, slow love again. This time each touched and tasted the spots that had been denied earlier; this time they both reached independent peaks before their

bodies finally joined. The lack of urgency that resulted
made the coming together and the leisurely climb and cul-
mination all the more meaningful. Though their bodies
would give out in time, they knew, their emotional desire
was never-ending.

After talking, then listening to soft music for a while as
they gazed into the fire, they finally retired to Web's big bed.
When they fell asleep in each other's arms, they felt as satisfied as if they'd made love yet again.

Saturday was a sterling day, one to be remembered by
them both for a long time to come. They slept late, awoke
to make love, then devoured a hearty brunch in the kitchen.
Though the snow had stopped sometime during the night,
the fresh inch or two on top of the existing crust gave a
crispness, a cleanness to the hilly woodlands surrounding
the cabin.

Bundled warmly against the cold, they took a long walk
in the early afternoon. It didn't matter that Marni couldn't
begin to make out a path; Web knew the woods by heart,
and she trusted him completely.

"So beautiful . . ." Her breath was a tiny cloud, evapo-
rating in the dry air as she looked around her. Tall pines
towered above, their limbs made all the more regal by the
snowy epaulets they wore. Underfoot the white carpet was
patterned, not only by the footprints behind them and the
tracks of birds and other small forest creatures, but by the
swish of low-hanging branches in the gentle breeze and the
fall of powdery clumps from branches. The silence was so
reverent across the mountainside that she felt intrusive even
when she murmured in awe, "Don't you wish you had a
camera?"

It had been a totally innocent question, an unpremedi-
tated one. Realizing the joke in it, Marni grinned up at Web.
"That was really dumb. You *do* have a camera . . . cameras.

I'd have thought you'd be out here taking pictures of everything."

He smiled back at her, thoroughly relaxed. "It's too peaceful."

"But it's beautiful!"

"A large part of that beauty is being here with you."

She gave a playful tug at the arm hers was wrapped around. "Flattery, flattery—"

"But I'm serious. Look around you now and try to imagine that you were alone, that we didn't have each other, that you were here on the mountain running away from some horrible threat or personal crisis. . . . How would you feel?"

"Cold."

"Y'see? People see things differently depending on where they're coming from. Right now I'm exactly where I want to be. I don't think I've ever felt as happy or content in my life. So you're right, this scene is absolutely beautiful."

Standing on tiptoe, she kissed his cheek, then tightened her arm through his. "Do you ever photograph up here?"

He shrugged. "I don't have a camera up here."

"You're kidding."

"Nope. This is my getaway. I knew from the first that if I allowed myself to bring a camera here, it wouldn't be a true escape."

"But you love photography, don't you?"

"I love my work, but photography in and of itself has never become an obsession with me. I've met some colleagues, both men and women, whose cameras are like dog tags around their necks. It gives them their identity. I've never wanted that. The camera is the tool of my trade, much like a calculator or computer is for an accountant, or a hammer is for a carpenter. Have you ever seen a carpenter go away for the weekend with his tool belt strapped around

his waist just in case he sees a nail sticking out on someone's house or on the back wall of a restaurant?"

Marni grinned. "No, I guess I haven't.... Why are you
looking at me that way?"

"You just look so pretty, all bundled up and rosy-cheeked.
You look as happy and content as I feel. I almost wish I did
have a camera, but I'm not sure I could begin to capture
what you are. Some things are better left as very special
images in the mind." He grew even more pensive.

"What is it?" she asked softly.

"Impulse time. Can I do it, too?"

"Sure. What's your impulse?"

"To photograph you out here in the woods. In the summer. Stark naked."

She quivered in excitement. "That's a naughty impulse."

"But that's not all." His blue eyes were glowing. "I'd like
to photograph you in bed right after we've made love. You're
all rosy-cheeked then too, and naked, but bundled up in
love."

She draped her arms over his shoulders. "Mmmm. I like
that one."

"But that's not all."

"There's more?"

"Uh-huh." His arms circled her waist. "I'd like to photograph you in bed right after we've made love. You're naked and rosy and wrapped in love. And you're pregnant.
You're breasts are fuller, with tiny veins running over them,
and your belly is round, the skin stretched tightly, protectively over our child."

Marni sucked in her breath and buried her face against
the fleece lining of his collar. "That's . . . beautiful, Web."

"But that's not all."

She gave a plaintive moan. "I'm not sure I can take much
more of this. My legs feel like water."

"Then I'll support you." True to his words, he tightened his arms around her. "I'd like to photograph you with our child at your breast. It could be a little Brian, or a little girl named Sunshine or Bliss or Liberty—"

She looked sharply up in mock rebuke. "You wouldn't."

"Wouldn't photograph you breast-feeding our child? You bet your sweet—"

"Wouldn't name the poor thing Sunshine or Bliss or Liberty. Do you have any idea what she'd go through, saddled with any one of those names?"

"Then you choose the name. Anything your heart desires."

Marni thought for a minute. "I kind of like Alana, or Arielle, or Amber—no, not Amber. It doesn't go well with Webster."

"You're partial to *A*'s?"

She tipped up her chin. "Nope. Just haven't gotten to the *B*'s yet."

She never did get to the *B*'s because he hugged her, and she was momentarily robbed of breath. When he released her long enough to loop his arm through hers again and start them along the path once more, he was thinking of things besides children. "We could keep your place if you'd like. Mine above the studio wouldn't be as appropriate for the entertaining you have to do."

"I don't know about that. It might spice things up. If we were really doing something big, we could use the studio itself, or rent space at a restaurant. I think I'd like the idea of knowing you'd be there whenever I came home from work."

"Would you have to travel much?"

"I could cut it down."

"I'd feel lonely when you were away."

"Maybe you could come." Her eyes lit up. "I mean, if I knew far enough in advance so that you could rearrange your schedule, we could take care of my business and have a vacation for ourselves."

"With Brian or Arielle or whoever?"

"By ourselves. Two adults doing adult things. We'd leave the baby with a sitter.... Uh-oh, that could be one drawback about living above your studio. You wouldn't get much work done with a squalling baby nearby."

"Are you kidding? I'd love it! I mean, we would hire someone to take care of the baby, and no baby of ours is going to be squalling all the time. I'd be able to see him or her during breaks or when the sitter was passing through the studio going out for walks. I'd be proud as punch to show off my child. And I'd be right there in case of any problem or emergency."

"But you shoot on location sometimes."

"Less and less in the last year or so, and I've reached the stage where I could cut it out entirely if I wanted to. Just think of it. It'd be an ideal situation." His cheeks were ruddy, and his blue eyes sparkled.

"You really mean that, don't you?"

"You bet. I never knew my own father. I want to know my children and have them know me."

"Child*ren?* Oh, boy, how many are we having?"

"Two, maybe three. More if you'd like, but I'd hate to think of your being torn between your work and a whole brood of kids. I'm told that working mothers suffer a certain amount of guilt even with one child."

He was right, but she couldn't resist teasing him. "Who told you that?"

He shrugged. "I read."

"What?"

"Oh . . . lots of things."

She couldn't contain a grin. His cheeks were a dead give-away, suddenly redder in a way that couldn't be from the cold. "Women's magazines?"

"Hell, my photographs are in them. Okay, sometimes one article or another catches my eye."

"And how long have you been reading about working mothers?"

"One article, Marni, that's it. It was—I don't know—maybe six or seven months ago."

"Did you know then that you wanted to have kids?"

"I've known for a long time, and when I read the article it was simply to satisfy an abstract curiosity." Smoothly, and with good humor, he took the offensive. "And you should be grateful that I *do* read. I'm thinking of you, sweet. Anything I've learned will make things easier for you."

"I'm not worried," she hummed, with a smile on her face.

They continued to walk, neither of them bothered by the cold air, if even aware of it. They were wrapped up in their world of dreams, a warm world where the sun was shining brightly. They talked of what they'd do in their leisure time, where they'd travel for vacations, what their children might be when they grew up.

The mood continued when they returned to the cabin. Marni sat on a barrel in the carport watching Web split logs for the fire. He sat on a stool in the kitchen watching her prepare a chicken-and-broccoli casserole. They sat by the fire talking of politics, the economy and foreign affairs, dreaming on, kissing, making love. Arms and legs entwined, they slept deeply that night—a good thing, because Sunday morning they awoke with the knowledge that before the day was through they'd be back in the real world facing those problems neither of them had been willing to discuss before.

Web lay in bed, staring at the ceiling. Marni was in a nearly identical position by his side. They'd been awake for a while, though neither had spoken. A thick quilt covered them, suddenly more necessary than it had seemed all weekend, for now they were thinking of an aspect of the future that was chilling to them both.

"What are we going to do about your parents, Marni?" Web asked. He'd contemplated approaching the topic gradually, but now he saw no point in beating around the bush.

She didn't twist her head in surprise, or even blink. "I don't know."

"What will they say if you announce that we're getting married?"

"Married. Funny. . . we haven't used that word before."

He tipped his head to look at her. "It was taken for granted, wasn't it?"

She met his gaze and spoke softly. "Yes."

"And you want it, don't you?"

"Yes."

"So—" his gaze drifted away "—what will they say?"

"They'll hit the roof."

He nodded, then swallowed. "How will you feel about that?"

"Pretty sick."

"It bothers you what they think?"

"Of course it does. They're my parents."

"You're not a child. You're old enough to make your own decisions."

"I know that, and I do make my own decisions every day of the week. This, well, this is a little tougher."

"Many adults have differences with their parents."

"But there are emotional issues here, very strong emotional issues."

"They blame me for Ethan's death."

"They blame you for everything that happened that summer."

"But mostly for Ethan's death." He sat up abruptly and turned to her, feelings he'd held in for years suddenly splintering outward. "Don't they know it was an accident? Those two cars collided and began spinning all over the road. There was no possible way I could have steered clear. Hell, we were wearing helmets, but a motorcycle didn't have any more of a chance against either of those monsters than Ethan's neck had against that tree."

Marni was lying stiffly, determined to say it all now. "It was your motorcycle. They felt that if Ethan had been with anyone else he would have been in a car and survived."

Frustrated, Web thrust his fingers through his hair. "I didn't force Ethan to come with me. For that matter, I didn't force Ethan to become my friend."

"But you were friends. My parents blame that on you, too."

"They saw their son as wasting his time with a no-good bum like me. Well, they were wrong, damn it! They were wrong! My friendship with Ethan was good for *both* of us. Ethan got a helluva lot more from me than he was getting from those other guys he hung around with, and I got more from him than you could ever believe. My, God! He was my friend! Do you think I wasn't crushed by his death?"

Tears glistened on his lower lids. Marni saw them and couldn't look away. She wanted to hold him, to comfort him, but at the moment there was a strange distance between them. She was a Lange. She was one of *them*.

"Y'know, Marni," he began in a deep voice that shook, "I lay in that hospital room bleeding on the inside long after they'd stitched me up on the outside. I hurt in ways no drug could ease. Yes, I felt guilty. It was my motorcycle, and I was driving, and if I'd been going a little faster or a little slower we would have missed that accident and been safe.... I called your father from the hospital. Did you know that?"

Eyes glued to his, she swallowed. "No."

"Well, I did. The day after the accident, when I'd been out from under the anesthetic long enough to be able to lift the phone. It was painful, lifting that phone. I had three cracked ribs, and my thigh was shattered into so many pieces that it had taken five hours of surgery to make some order out of it—and that's not counting the two operations that followed. But nothing, *nothing* I felt physically could begin to compare with the pain your father inflicted on me. He didn't ask how I was, didn't stop to think that I was hurting or that I was torn up by the knowledge that Ethan had died and I was alive. No, all he asked was whether I was satisfied, whether I was pleased I'd destroyed a life that would have been so much more meaningful, so much more productive than mine had ever been or could be."

An anger rose in Marni, so great that she could no longer bear the thought of presenting her parents' side of the story. She sat up and moved to Web, her own eyes flooding as she curled her hands around his neck. "He had no right to say that! It *wasn't* your fault! I told him that over and over again, but he wouldn't listen to me. I was an irresponsible seventeen-year-old who'd been stupid to have been involved with you, he said. That showed how much *I* knew."

Web dragged in a long, shaky breath. He was looking at her, but not actually seeing her. His vision was on the past. "I cried. I lay there holding the phone and cried. The nurse finally came in and took it out of my hand, but I kept on crying until I was so tired and in so much pain that I just couldn't cry anymore."

She brushed at the moisture in the corners of his eyes, though his face was blurred to her gaze. "I'm so sorry, Web," she whispered. "So sorry. He was wrong, and cruel. There was nothing you could have done to prevent that accident. It wasn't your fault!"

"But I felt guilty. I still do."

"What about me?" she cried. "If it hadn't been for me—for my pestering the two of you to take me along—you would have been in Ethan's car as you'd originally planned. Don't you think that's haunted me all these years? I tried to tell that to my father, too, because it hurt so much when he put the full blame on you, but he wouldn't listen. All he could think of was that Ethan, his only son and primary heir, was gone. And my mother seconded everything he said, especially when he forbade me to see you again."

"What about Tanya? Didn't she come to your defense?"

"Tanya, who'd been itching for you from the first moment she knew we were involved with each other? No, Tanya didn't come to my defense. She told my mother everything she knew, about the times I'd said I was out with friends but was actually out with you. She was legitimately upset about Ethan, I have to say that much for her. But she did nothing to help me through what was a double devastation. She sided with my parents all the way."

Marni hung her head. Tears stained her cheeks, and her hands clutched Web's shoulders for the solace that his muscled strength could offer. "I wanted to go to you, Web." Her voice was small and riddled with pain. "I kept thinking of you in that hospital, even when we returned to Long Island for the funeral. I wanted to go back to Maine to see you, because I needed to know you were okay and I needed your comfort. You'd meant so much to me that summer. I'd been in love with you, and I felt that you might be the only one to help me get over Ethan's death."

"But they wouldn't let you come."

"They said that if I made any move to contact you, they'd disinherit me. That if I tried to see you, they'd know that they'd failed as parents."

He smoothed her hair back around her ears, then said softly, "I waited. I was hoping you'd come, or call, because I thought maybe you could make me feel a little better about what had happened. I was in that godforsaken small-town hospital for two months—"

"How could I go against them?" she cried, trying desperately to justify what she'd done. "Regardless of how wrong they were about you, they were grief-stricken over Ethan. It wasn't the threat of being disinherited that bothered me. It wasn't a matter of money. But they'd given me everything for seventeen years. You'd given me other things, but for barely two months." She took a quick breath. "You said that you thought I was headstrong in my way even then, but I wasn't really, Web. I couldn't stand up for something I wanted. I'd already disappointed my parents. I couldn't do it again. They were going through too rough a time. Dad was never the same after the accident."

Web's expression had softened, and his voice was tinged with regret. "None of us were. That accident was the turning point in my life." His words hung, heavy and profound, in the air for a minute. Then he turned, propped the pillows against the headboard and settled Marni against him as he leaned back. "My leg kept getting infected and wouldn't heal, so I was transferred to a place in Boston. The specialist my stepfather found opened the whole thing up and practically started from scratch again, and between that and a second, less extensive operation, I was hospitalized for another six weeks. I had lots of time to think. Lots of time.

"Ethan and I, I realized, each represented half of an ideal world. He had financial stability, but though many of the things he had told me about in those hours we spent together sounded wonderful, they didn't come free. I had freedom and a sense of adventure, but without roots or money I was limited as to what I could do in life. As I lay there, I thought a lot about my father and about why I'd been running, and it was then I realized I wanted something more in life. Your parents thought I was dirt, and I felt like it after the accident. But I didn't want to be dirt. I wanted to be *someone*, not just a jock moving from job to job and place to place." He stroked her arm as though needing to reassure himself that he'd found a measure of personal stability at last.

"What happened to Ethan made me think about my own mortality," he went on in a solemn voice. "If I'd died then and there, no one—well, other than my immediate family—would have missed me, and it was questionable as to whether they'd really miss me, since I'd never been around all that much." He took a deep breath. "So I hooked onto that dig in New Mexico. It was the first time I'd ever done something with an eye toward the future. By the time I realized I'd never make it as a writer, my pictures were selling. I was on my way. I don't think anything could have stopped me from pushing ahead full steam at that point."

Marni, who'd been listening quietly, raised her face to his. "You've done Ethan proud. He gave you the motivation, and you worked your way up from scratch to become very successful."

Web was studying her tenderly. "And what about you? You've done much of what you have for him, too, haven't you?"

"For him . . . and my parents." She rushed on before he could argue. "I grieved so long after the accident, for both Ethan and you, and the sadness and guilt I felt were getting me nowhere. I decided that the only way I could redeem myself was to make my parents proud of me. Yes, I've tried to fill Ethan's shoes. I'm sure I haven't done it in the same way he would have, but I do think I've filled a certain void for my parents. After Ethan's death, Dad began to lose interest in the business. My decision to enter it was like a shot in the arm for him. Of course shots wear off after a while, and he eased away from the corporation earlier than he might have, but by then I was trained and ready to take over."

"You felt you were making up to your parents for having played a small part in Ethan's death."

Her whispered "Yes" was barely audible, but a shudder passed through Web, and he held her tightly to him.

"We've both suffered. We paid the fine for what we'd done, or thought we'd done, but the suffering isn't over if your parents are going to stand between us." They'd come full stride. "What are we going to do about them, Marni?"

"I don't know," she murmured, teeth gritted against the helplessness that assailed her. "I don't know."

"We'll have to tell them. We'll have to present ourselves and our best arguments to them—"

"Not 'we.' It'd never work that way, Web. They'd never listen. Worse, they'd kick you out of the house. It'd be better if I spoke with them first. I could break it to them gently."

"God, it's like we've committed some kind of crime."

"In their minds we have. What I've done will be tantamount to treason in their minds."

"They'll just have to change their way of thinking."

"That's easier said than done."

"What other choice will they have? They can't very well kick their own grown-up daughter out of the house. And then there's the matter of the corporation presidency. Your father may be chairman of the board, but no board worth its salt is going to evict its president simply because she falls in love with someone her father doesn't like. You've done a good job, Marni. You've invaluable to the corporation."

"Not invaluable. Certainly not indispensable. But I'm not really worried about anything happening at work. Dad wouldn't go *that* far. What I fear most is what will happen at home. Ethan's death left a gaping hole. Every time the family got together, we were aware of his absence. If Mom and Dad push us away because of my relationship with you, the unit will be that much weaker. If they could only reconcile themselves to gaining a son, rather than losing a daughter..."

"Reconcile. A powerful word."

Marni was deep in thought. "Mmmm.... What if I break it to them gently? Mother hasn't made the connection between you and that other Web. Apparently neither has Dad, since he didn't make a peep over the plans to use you as cover photographer for *Class*. What if I were to tell them that we were dating, that I was seeing the photographer and that we were pretty serious about each other?"

"They'd want to meet me. One look and they'd know."

"We could stall them. After all, I'm busy, and so are you, which would make it hard to arrange a meeting. In the meantime I could tell them all about Brian Webster, show them examples of your work and snow them with lists of your credits. I could create a picture in their minds of everything you are and everything you mean to me."

"And they won't ask about my background?" He knew very well they would.

"I could fudge it, be as vague as I like. Then, when they've got this super image in their minds, when they're as favorably inclined as possible, I could tell them the rest."

He raised her chin with his forefinger. "A super image can shatter with a few short words. What if, in spite of the advance hype, they go off the deep end?"

His eyes were a mirror of hers. Marni saw there the same trepidation, the same worry that was making her insides knot. "Then I'll have to make a choice," she said at last.

The trepidation, the worry were transferred to his voice, which came out in a tremulous whisper. Once before Marni had had a choice to make, and she'd made it in favor of her family. Web felt that his very life was on the line. "What will you choose?" he asked in a raw whisper.

Neither her eyes, lost in his, nor her voice faltered. "You're my future, Web. I'm grateful for everything they've given me, and I do love them, but you're my future. The love I feel for you is so strong that there's really no choice at all."

Web closed his eyes. His sigh fanned her brow, and his arms tightened convulsively around her. "Oh, baby..." He said nothing more but held her, rocking her, savoring the moment, the joy, the intense relief he felt.

Inevitably, though, the ramifications of what she'd said loomed before him. "It's going to be hard. You'll be upset."

"Yes. It's sad that I have to risk alienating them by telling them that I'm—"

"—marrying the guy who killed their son."

Her head shot up, eyes flashing in anger. "You *didn't* kill Ethan. Don't ever say that again!"

He felt compelled to prepare her. "They'll say it."

"And they'll be wrong again. They may have used you for a scapegoat that summer, they may be doing it still, and I suppose it's only natural that parents try to find someone to blame, some reason to explain a tragedy like that. But, damn it, you've been their scapegoat long enough!"

"You're apt to take over that role, if it comes down to an estrangement."

"Oh, Web, Web, let's not assume the worst until we come to it . . . please?"

THEY LEFT THE DISCUSSION on that pleading note, but the rest of the day was nowhere near as carefree as the day before had been. They breakfasted, walked again through the woods, packed their bags and closed up the house, all the while struggling to elude the dark cloud hovering overhead.

An atmosphere of apprehension filled the car during the drive back to the city. Web clutched her hand during most of the trip, knowing the dread she was feeling and in turn being swamped by helplessness and frustration. At the door of her apartment, he hugged her with a kind of desperation.

"I'm so afraid of losing you, sunshine . . . so afraid. I was a fool fourteen years ago for not realizing what I had, but I'm not a fool anymore. I'm going to fight, Marni. I'm going to fight, if it's the last thing I do!"

Those words, and the love behind them, were to be a much-needed source of strength for Marni in the days to come.

7

MARNI HAD HAD EVERY INTENTION on Monday of calling her mother about the wonderful weekend she'd had with Brian Webster, but she didn't seem to find the time. When, as prearranged, Web came to take her to dinner that night, she explained that something had come up in the computer division, demanding her attention for most of the day. She'd had little more than a moment here or there to think of making the call.

On Tuesday it was a problem with the proposed deal in Richmond, one she thought she'd ironed out when she'd gone down there the week before. On Wednesday it was a lawsuit, filed against the corporation's publishing division by one of its authors.

"You're hedging," Web accused when he saw her that night.

"I'm not! These things came up, and I need a free mind when I call her."

"Things are always coming up. It's the nature of your work. You can put off that call forever, but it's not going to solve our problem."

"Speaking of problems, what are we going to do about the cover of *Class*?" She knew the second batch of pictures had been better than the first, but that Web was still not fully satisfied.

"You're changing the subject."

"Maybe, but it is a problem, and we both do have a deadline on that one."

"We've got a deadline on both, if you look at it one way. The longer you put off breaking the news about us to your parents, the longer it'll be before we can get married."

"I know," she whispered, looking down at the fingernail she was picking. "I know."

Web knew she was torn, that she loved him and wanted to marry him, but that she was terrified of what her parents' reaction was going to be. He sympathized, but only to a point.

"I'll make a deal with you," he sighed. "I'll study all the proofs and decide what to do about them, if you call your mother. . . . Sound fair?"

"Of course it's fair," she snapped. He was right. She was only prolonging the inevitable. "I'll call her tomorrow."

SHE DID BETTER than that. Fearful that she'd lose her nerve when the time came, she called her mother that night and invited her to lunch. It was over coffee and trifle, the latter barely touched on her plate, that Marni broached the subject.

"Mother, do you remember that photographer I was with that night we witnessed the assault?"

Adele Lange, a slender woman with a surprisingly sweet tooth, was relishing every small forkful of wine-soaked sponge cake, fruit, nuts and whipped cream that made up the trifle. She held her fork suspended. "Of course I remember." She smiled. "He's the famous one everyone knows about but me."

Marni forced her own smile as she launched into the speech she'd mentally rehearsed so many times. "Well, we've been dating. I think it's getting serious."

Adele stared at her, then set down her fork. "But I thought you said it was a business thing."

"It started out that way, but it's evolved into something more." So far, the truth. Marni kept her chin up.

"Marni! It's been—how long—a week since that incident? How many times could you have seen this man to know that it's getting serious?"

"I'm thirty-one, Mom. I know."

"Does he? Remember what I told you about photographers?"

"You're hung up on the stereotype. You've never met Brian."

"Then tell me. What's he like?" Slowly Adele returned to her trifle, but she was clearly distracted.

"He's tall, dark and handsome, for starters."

"Aren't they all?"

"No. Some are squat and wiry-haired—"

"And wear heavy gold jewelry, have their eyes on every attractive woman in sight and can't make it through a sentence without a 'darling' or 'sweetie' or 'babe.'"

Marni grinned. "Brian doesn't use any of those words. He doesn't wear any jewelry except a watch, which is slim and unobtrusive, and he may have the same appreciation that any other man his age has for a beautiful woman, but he's never looked at another woman the way he looks at me." Nicely put, Marni thought, almost poetic. She'd have to remember that one.

"How old is he?"

"Forty."

"And he's never married?"

"No."

"That's something strange to think about. Why hasn't he married? A man who's got looks and a name for himself . . . maybe he's queer."

If Marni had had a mouthful of coffee, she would have choked on it. It was all she could do to keep a straight face. "Would he be interested in me if he was?"

Adele's lips twitched downward in disdain. "Maybe he goes both ways."

"He doesn't. Take my word for it."

"And you take his word that he doesn't have an ex-wife or two to support?"

"He's never been married," Marni stated unequivocably, then took a sip of her coffee. She knew her mother. The questions were just beginning. She only wished they would all be as amusing.

"Where does he come from?"

"Pennsylvania, originally."

Adele took another tiny forkful of trifle. "What about his parents?"

"His mother is dead. His father is an insurance broker." She'd anticipated the question and had thought about the answer she'd give. To say "stepfather" would only be to invite questions. Web had never known his biological father, hence Marni felt justified in responding as she did.

Adele was chewing and swallowing each bit of information along with the trifle. "How long has he been a photographer?"

"He's been at it since his mid-twenties."

"I assume, given the reputation Tanya claims he has, that he earns a good living."

"What kind of a question is that, Mother?"

"It's a mother's kind of question."

"I'm an independent adult. I earn a more than comfortable salary for myself. Why should it matter what W—what Brian earns?" The sudden skip of her heart hadn't been caused by her indignation. She'd nearly slipped. Brian was a safe name; Web was not. She'd have to be more careful.

Adele scolded her gently. "Don't get upset, darling. For the first time in your adult life, you've told me that you're serious about a man. Your father and I have waited a long time for this. It's only natural that we be concerned about whether he's right for you. Realistically speaking, you're a wealthy woman. We wouldn't want to think that some man was interested in you for your money."

Farcical. That was what it was, and Marni couldn't help but laugh. "No, Brian is *not* interested in my money. Not that it matters, but he's far from being a pauper. He has an extremely lucrative career, he owns the building that houses his studio and his apartment and he's got a weekend home on acres of woodland in Vermont." She hesitated, wondering just how much to say, then decided to throw caution aside. "We were there last weekend. It's beautiful."

Adele's eyes widened fractionally, and she pursed her lips, but said nothing about Marni's having spent the weekend with her photographer. Marni was, after all, thirty-one, and these were modern times. It was too much to expect that her daughter was still a virgin. "Vermont. A little... backwoodsy, isn't it?"

Marni rolled her eyes. "Vermont has become the vacation place of most of New York, or hadn't you noticed? Some of the finest and wealthiest have second homes there. Times have changed, Mother. It doesn't have to be Camden, or South Hampton, or Newport anymore."

"I know that, darling," Adele said gruffly. She scowled at what was left of her dessert, then abandoned it in favor of her coffee.

"I want you to be *pleased*," Marni said softly. "Brian is a wonderful man. He's interesting and fun to be with, he's serious about his work and he respects mine, and he treats me like I'm the best thing that's ever happened to him."

"I am pleased. I just want to make sure you know what you're doing before you get in over your head."

Marni might have said that she was already in over her head, but it wouldn't have served her purpose. "I know what I'm doing," she said with quiet conviction. "I'm happy. That's the most important thing . . . don't you think?"

"Of course, dear. Of course. . . . So, when will we be able to meet this photographer of yours?"

"Soon."

"When?"

"When I get up the courage to bring him out."

"Courage? Why would you need courage?"

"Because you and Dad can be intimidating in the best of circumstances. I'm not sure I'm ready to inflict you on Brian yet." Her words had been offered in a teasing tone and accompanied by a gentle smile. Adele was totally unaware of the deeper sentiment behind them.

"Very funny, Marni. We don't bite you know."

"You could send Brian running if you grill him the way you've grilled me. No man likes to have his background, his social standing and his financial status probed."

"Social standing. We haven't even gotten into that."

"No need. He's well-liked and respected, he's the good friend of many well-placed people and he chews with his mouth closed."

"That's a relief," was Adele's sardonic retort. "I wouldn't want to think you were going with some crude oaf."

"Brian can hold his own with any crowd. He'll charm your friends to tears."

"Well, *your father and I* would like to meet him before we introduce him to our friends. Why don't you bring him out to the house on Sunday?"

Marni shook her head. "We're not up to a showing just yet."

"If you're so afraid that we'll scare the man off, maybe you're not so sure about him yourself."

"Oh, I'm sure. But it's still a little early for introductions," she explained with impeccable nonchalance. "When the time's right, I'll let you know."

"YOU WOULD HAVE BEEN PROUD of me, Web," Marni declared when she arrived at the studio that night. Web had kissed her thoroughly. She was feeling heavenly. "I was cool and relaxed, I followed the script perfectly and I didn't lie once."

"How did she take it?"

"Hesitantly, at first. She asked questions, just as I'd expected." She told him some of them, and they shared a chuckle over the one about money. "I planted the bug in her ear. If I know my mother, she's already on the phone trying to find out whatever she can about you." A sudden frown crossed her brow. Web picked up on it instantly.

"Don't worry. There's nothing she could learn that will connect me with who I was fourteen years ago. Lee is about the only one who knows anything about what I did during those years, and even if someone called him, which they wouldn't, he'd be tight-lipped as hell."

"He must think my parents are awful."

"Not awful. Just . . . prejudiced."

"Mmmm. I guess that says it." Her eyes clouded. "It remains to be seen whether they're vengeful as well."

"Don't even think it," Web soothed. "Not yet. We've got more pressing things to consider."

"More pressing?" she asked, worried. But Web was grinning, drawing her snugly against him. "Ahhh. More pressing . . ."

His lips closed over hers then, and soon he was leading her to the bedroom, where he proceeded to set her priorities straight. It was what she needed, what they both needed—a reaffirmation of all they meant to each other. Passion was a ready spark between them, had always been a ready spark between them, but it was love that dominated the interplay of mouths and hands and bodies, and it was love that transported them to an exquisite corner of paradise.

MARNI'S FATHER DROPPED BY her office on Friday morning. She was surprised to see him, because there wasn't a board meeting scheduled and he rarely came in for anything else. But deep down inside she'd been awaiting some form of contact.

They talked of incidental things relating to the corporation, and Marni indulged him patiently. In his own good time, Jonathan Lange broached the topic that had brought him by. His thick brows were low over his eyes.

"Your mother tells me that you have a special man...this photographer...Brian Webster?"

"Uh-huh." Her pulse rate had sped up, but she kept her eyes and her voice steady and forcefully relaxed her hands in her lap.

"I know your mother has some reservations," he went on in his most businesslike tone, "and I hope you take them seriously. People today get married, then divorced, married, then divorced. Your sister is a perfect example."

"I'm not Tanya," Marni stated quietly.

"Exactly. You're the president of this corporation. I hope you keep that in mind when you go about choosing a husband."

She had to struggle to contain a surge of irritation. "I know who I am, Dad, and I think I have a pretty good grasp of what's expected of me."

"Just so you do. This fellow's a photographer, and big-name photographers often live in the fast lane. I wouldn't want you—or him—to do anything to embarrass us."

Embarrassment had never been among Marni's many worries. "I think you're jumping the gun," she said slowly. "In the first place, you've adopted the same stereotype Mom has. There's nothing fast about Brian. He lives quietly, and his face hasn't been plastered all over the papers, with or without women." Web had assured her of that. All she'd needed was for her mother or Tanya to do a little sleuthing and come up with a picture that would identify Web instantly. "Furthermore, I don't believe I said anything to Mom about marriage."

Jonathan's frown was one of reproof. "Then you'd move in with the man, without a thought to your image?"

"Come on, Dad. These are enlightened times. No one cares if two adults choose to live together."

"Is that what *you* choose?"

"No! I've never even considered it."

"But you haven't talked marriage with this photographer?"

That one was harder to fudge. She bought a minute's time. "His name is Brian. You can call him Brian."

"All right. Brian. Have you talked marriage with Brian?"

She held his gaze. "I think we'd both be amenable to the idea."

"Then it *is* serious."

"Yes."

"We'll have to meet him. That's all there is to it."

Marni bit her lower lip, then let it slide from beneath her teeth. "You know, Dad, I am a big girl. Technically, I don't need your approval. You may hate him, but that wouldn't change my feelings for him."

Jonathan's gaze sharpened. "If he's as wonderful as you say, why would we hate him?"

"Different people see things differently. You and Mom aren't keen on his profession to begin with."

"That's true. But we'd still like to meet him, and soon, if you're as serious as you say about him."

"Okay, soon. You will meet him soon."

THERE WAS SOON, and there was soon. Marni had no intention of running out to Long Island that Sunday as her mother had originally suggested. Not only did she have more subtle PR to do, but she and Web were going back to Vermont for the weekend, and not for the world would she have altered their plans.

They had a relaxed, quiet, loving weekend and returned to New York refreshed and anticipating the next step in Marni's plan. On Monday she sent her parents tear sheets of the best of Web's work. Each piece was identified as to where it had appeared; it was an impressive collection of credits. She also sent along copies of blurbs and articles praising Web's work.

On Monday night she and Web took in a movie. On Tuesday they went out to dinner. On Wednesday morning she called her mother as a follow-up to the package she'd sent. Yes, Adele had received it, and, yes, it was an impressive lot. Yes, Marni was planning to bring him out to the house, but, no, it couldn't be this week because they were both swamped with work.

Marni and Web spent a quiet Wednesday night at her place, then a similarly quiet Thursday night at his. After the full days they put in at their respective jobs, they found these private times to be most precious.

Friday night, though, they had a party to attend. It was given by the most recently named vice-president at Lange,

Heather Connolly, whom Marni had personally recruited from another company four years before.

Had the party been an official corporate function, Marni might have thought twice about bringing Web along. She felt she was progressing well with her parents and wouldn't have done anything to jeopardize her plan. But the party was a personal one, a gathering of the Connollys' friends. Marni was looking forward to it; it was the first time she would be introducing Web to any of her own friends.

They had fun dressing up, Web in a dark, well-tailored suit, Marni in a black sequined cocktail dress. It was a miracle they noticed anyone else at the party, so captivated were they by each other's appearance. But they did manage to circulate, talking easily with Heather and Fred's friends, their spouses and dates.

At ten o'clock, though, the unthinkable happened. A couple arrived: the man a tennis partner of Fred's, the woman none other than Marni's sister, Tanya.

Marni was the first to see them. She and Web were chatting with another couple when they entered the room. Her heart began to pound, and she stiffened instantly. Instinctively she reached for Web's arm and dug in her fingers. He took one look at her ashen face, followed her gaze and stared.

"Tanya?" he whispered in disbelief. It had been fourteen years, but he would have recognized her even had Marni's reaction not been a solid clue. Clearing his throat, he turned smoothly back to the couple. "Would you excuse us? Marni's sister has just come. We hadn't expected to see her." Without awaiting more than nods from the two, he guided Marni toward the back of the room, ostensibly to circle the crowd toward Tanya.

Marni's whisper was as frantic as she felt. "What are we *going to do*? She'll recognize you! She's *sure* to recognize you, and she's trouble! Oh, God, Web, what do we do?"

He positioned himself so that his large body was a buffer between Marni and the rest of the crowd, then curved his fingers around her arms. "Take it easy. Just relax. There's not much we can do, Marni. If we try to slip out without being seen, our disappearance will cause an even greater stir. Tanya's not dumb. She'll put two and two together, and if she's the troublemaker you say, she'll run right back to your parents. The damage will be done anyway." He paused. "The best thing, the *only* thing we can do is to walk confidently up and say hello."

Marni's eyes were wide with dismay. "But she'll *recognize* you."

"Probably."

"But . . . that'll be awful!"

"It'll just bring things to a head a little sooner."

"Web, I don't want this . . . I don't want this!"

He slipped to her side, put his arm around her shoulder and spoke very gently. "Let's get it over with. The sooner the better. Take a deep breath . . . atta girl . . . now smile."

She tried, but the best she could muster was a feeble twist of her lips.

Web gave a tight smile of his own. "That'll have to do." He took his own deep breath. "Let's go."

Tanya and her date were talking with Heather and Fred when they approached. "Marni," Heather exclaimed, "look who's here! I never dreamed Tony would be bringing Tanya. Do you and Brian know Tony? Tony Holt, Marni Lange and Brian Webster."

Marni forced a smile in Tanya's direction. "Hi, Tanya." She clutched Web's arm. "I don't think you know Brian."

Tanya hadn't taken her eyes from Web since she'd turned at their approach. Her face, too, had paled, and there was a hint of shock in her eyes, but otherwise her expression was socially perfect. She extended a formal hand. "Brian . . . Webster, is it?"

If she'd put special emphasis on his last name, only Marni and Web were aware of it. Two things were instantly clear— first, that she did *indeed* know Brian and, second, that she was momentarily going along with the game.

Web took her hand in his own firm one. "It's a pleasure to meet you, Tanya."

"My pleasure entirely," was Tanya's silky response. The underlying innuendo was, again, obvious only to Web and Marni.

Web shook hands with Tony Holt, who, it turned out, was a plastic surgeon very familiar with his photographic work. Reluctantly, since he'd rather have been helping Marni, Web was drawn into conversation with the man. Heather and Fred moved off. Tanya seized Marni's arm. "We'll be in the powder room, Tony." She winked at her date. "Be right back."

Before Marni could think of a plausible excuse, she was being firmly led around the crowd and up the stairs to the second floor of the townhouse. Tanya said nothing until she'd found a bathroom and closed its door firmly behind them. Then she turned on Marni, hands on hips, eyes wide in fury.

"How could you! How could you *think* to do something like this to us! When I talked with Mom the other day, she told me you were serious about this Brian Webster. She didn't make the connection. *None* of us made the connection."

Marni refused to be intimidated. "The connection's unimportant."

"Unimportant? Have you lost your marbles?" Tanya raised a rigid finger and pointed to the door. "That man killed our brother, and you don't think the connection's important?"

"Brian did not . . . kill . . . Ethan," Marni stated through gritted teeth, her own fury quickly rising to match her sister's. "That accident was carefully documented by the police. Brian was in no way at fault."

Tanya sliced the air with her hand. "It doesn't matter what the police said. He was a bad influence on Ethan. If he hadn't come along that summer, Ethan would still be alive. Your *own brother*. How could you insult his memory by doing this?"

"Ethan liked and respected Web," Marni countered angrily. Quite unconsciously she'd reverted to calling Brian Web, but even if she'd thought about it, she'd have realized that there was no longer any need for pretense. "If he'd survived the accident, he'd have been the first one to say that Web wasn't at fault. And given the age that I am now, he'd have been the first to bless my relationship with Web."

"So you're desperate, is that it? You're thirty-one and single, and *that* man is your only hope?"

"Yes, that man is my only hope, but not because I'm thirty-one. I happen to love him. He fills needs I never realized I had."

"Very touching. Is that what you're going to say to Mom and Dad when they finally learn the truth? And when were you planning to tell them anyway? They're going to be thrilled, absolutely thrilled."

"Do you think I don't know that? Do you think I've been evasive simply to amuse myself? I'm finding no pleasure in this, Tanya, and the worst of it is that you people are making me feel guilty when I've got nothing to feel guilty about. I'd planned to tell Mom and Dad when the time was right.

I was hoping that they'd form an image of what Brian Webster is like today, to somehow counter the image they've held of him all these years."

"You're dreaming, little sister—"

"Don't call me little sister," Marni said in a warning tone. "We're both adults now. It doesn't seem to me...." She closed her mouth abruptly. She'd been about to say that Tanya hadn't done anything with her life that would give her the right, or authority, to look down on Marni, but she realized that insults would get her nowhere. Yes, Tanya would go to their parents with what she'd learned, and maybe Marni *was* dreaming, but there was always that chance, that slim chance Tanya could be an ally.

Marni took a deep breath and raised both hands in a truce. "What I could use, Tanya, is your help. It's going to be very difficult for Mom and Dad, because I know they share your feelings that Web was responsible for Ethan's death. They're older, and Ethan was their child. I was hoping you could see things more objectively."

Tanya's eyes flashed. "You are *not* going to marry that man."

"And it matters that much to you who I marry?" Marni asked softly.

"You can marry anyone you please as long as it's not him."

Marni looked down at her hands and chose her words with care. "Fourteen years ago, you wanted Web for yourself. Could that be coloring your opinion?"

"Of course not. I didn't want him for myself. I knew what kind of a person he was from the start."

Marni bit back a retort concerning both Tanya's erstwhile interest in Web and the character of her two ex-husbands. "Do you know what kind of a person he is now?" she asked quietly.

"It doesn't matter. When I look at him I can only remember what he did. Mom and Dad are going to do the same."

"But think. He has a good career. He's successful and well-liked. He doesn't have the slightest blemish on his record. Can you still stand there and claim he's a killer?"

Before Tanya could answer, a light knock came at the door, then Web's voice calling, "Marni?" Marni quickly opened the door. Web looked from one sister to the other, finally settling a more gentle gaze on Marni. "Is everything okay here?"

"No, it's not," Tanya answered in a huff. "If you had any sense, you'd get out of my sister's life once and for all."

Marni turned to her with a final plea. "Tanya, I could really use your help—"

"When hell freezes over. I wouldn't—"

"That's enough," Web interrupted with quiet determination. His voice softened, and he reached for Marni's hand. "We've got to run, Marni. I've already explained to Heather that I have to be up early tomorrow. She understands."

With all hope that Tanya might aid her dashed, Marni didn't look at her sister again. She took Web's hand and let him lead her down the stairs and quietly out of the townhouse. She leaned heavily against him as they began to walk. Yes, Web had to be up early tomorrow. So did she. They were heading for Vermont, where she wouldn't be able to hear her phone when it began to jangle angrily.

8

MARNI'S PARENTS weren't put off by the fact that she wasn't home to answer her phone. They quickly called her administrative assistant, who gave them Web's Vermont number.

It was shortly after two in the afternoon. Marni and Web had left New York early, had stopped at their usual market for food and were just finishing lunch. When the phone rang, they looked up in surprise, then at each other in alarm. In all the time they'd spent at the cabin, the phone hadn't rung once.

"Don't answer it," Marni warned. Neither of them had moved yet.

"It may not be them."

The phone rang a second time. "It is. We both know it is."

"It may be a legitimate emergency. What if one of them is sick?" He began to rise from his seat. The only phone was in the den.

Marni clutched his wrist, her eyes filled with trepidation. "Let it ring," she begged.

"They'll only keep trying. I won't have the weekend spoiled. If we let it ring, we'll keep wondering. But if we answer it, at least we'll know one way or another."

"The weekend will be spoiled anyway.... Web!"

He was on his way toward the den. She ran after him.

He lifted the receiver and spoke calmly. "Hello?"

A slightly gruff voice came from the other end of the line. "Marni Lange, please."

"Who's calling?"

". . . Her father."

As if Web hadn't known. He would have recognized that voice in any timbre. He'd last heard it when he'd been lying, distraught, in a hospital room.

"Mr. Lange—" Web began, not knowing what he was going to say, only knowing that he wanted to deflect from Marni the brunt of what was very obviously anger. He was curtly interrupted.

"My daughter, please."

Marni was at Web's elbow, trying to take the phone from him, but he resisted. "If this is something that concerns—"

"I'd like to *speak to my daughter*!"

Hearing her father's shout, Marni tugged harder on the phone. "Web, please . . ."

He held up his free hand to her, even as he spoke calmly into the receiver. "If you're angry, Mr. Lange, you're angry at me. Perhaps you ought to tell me what's on your mind."

"Are you going to put my daughter on the line?"

"Not yet."

Jonathan Lange hung up the phone.

Web heard the definitive click and took the phone from his ear, whereupon Marni snatched it to hers. "Dad? Hello? Dad?" She scowled at the receiver, then slammed it down. "Damn it, Web. You should have let me talk! What good does it do if he's hung up? Now nothing's accomplished!"

"Something is. Your father knows that I have no intention of letting you face this alone. You faced it alone fourteen years ago. I like to think I'm more of a man now."

"Then it's a macho thing?" she cried. "You're trying to show him who wears the pants around here?"

"Don't be absurd, Marni! Our relationship has been one of equals from the start. I simply want your father to know that we're standing together, that if he thinks he can browbeat you, he'll be browbeating both of us. And I don't take to being browbeaten."

"Then you'll shut every door as soon as it's opened. He *called. You* were the one who insisted on answering the phone. Now you've hung up on him—"

"He hung up on me!"

"Same difference—"

"No, it's not," Web argued angrily. "*He* shut the door. I was perfectly willing to talk."

"But he wouldn't talk with you, so now he's not talking with either of us."

"He'll call back. If he went to the effort of getting this number, he won't give up so easily."

"Then I'll answer it next time."

"And he'll bully you mercilessly. You've got to be firm with him, Marni! You've got to let him know that you're not a child who can be pushed around!"

"I'm *not* a child, and I don't like your suggestion that I am."

"I didn't suggest—"

"You don't trust me! You think I'm going to crumble. You think that I'll submit to every demand he makes. I told you I wouldn't, Web! I *told* you that my choice was made!"

"But you're torn, because you don't want to hurt them. Well, what about me? Don't I have a right to stand in my own defense? If he's going to call me a killer, it's my *right* to tell him where to get off!"

"But that won't accomplish anything!" she screamed, then caught her breath and held it. The silence was deafening, coming on the heels of their heated exchange. "Oh, God," she whimpered at last. She clutched his shoulders, then threw her arms around his neck and clung to him tightly. "Oh, God, he's doing it already. He's putting a wedge between us. Do you see what's happening? Do you see it, Web?"

His own arms circled her slowly, then closed in. Eyes squeezed shut, he buried his face in her hair. "I see, sweetheart. I see, and it makes me sick. If we start fighting about this, we'll never make it. And if *we* don't, *I* won't."

"Me neither," she managed shakily. "I love you so much, Web. It tears me up that you have to go through this, when you've already paid such a high price for something that wasn't your fault."

He rubbed soothing circles over her back. "That's neither here nor there at this point. I'm more than willing to go through hell if it means I'll get you in the end." His voice grew hoarse. "I don't know how I could have yelled at you that way. You're not responsible for the situation any more than I am."

The phone rang again. A jolt passed from one body to the other. Marni raised her face and looked questioningly at Web, who held her gaze for a minute before stepping back and nodding toward the phone.

Marni lifted the receiver. "Hello?"

"Marni!" It was her mother. "Thank goodness it's you this time! Your father is ready to—"

Cutting her off, Jonathan came on the line. "What do you think you're doing, Marni?" he demanded harshly. "Do you know who that man is?"

She felt surprisingly calm. Anticipation had prepared her well. With the moment at hand, she was almost relieved. "I certainly do. He's the man I'm going to marry." She reached for Web's hand and held it to her middle.

"Over my dead body!" came the retort. "Do you have any idea what this has done to your mother and me? You were very cagey, telling us everything about this Brian Webster of yours but his real identity. If Tanya hadn't called—"

"Everything I told you was the truth."

"Don't interrupt me, Marni. You may be the president of the corporation, but in this house you're still the baby."

"I am not still in that house, and I am *not* still the baby! I'm a grown woman, Dad. Isn't it about time you accepted that?"

"I had, until you pulled this little stunt. Are you out of your mind? Do you have any *idea* how I feel about this?"

Marni took a deep breath in a bid for calm. She had to be able to think clearly and project conviction. A glance at Web gave her strength a boost. "Yes, I think I do. I also think that you're wrong. But I won't be able to convince you of it over the phone."

"Damned right you won't. I'd suggest you get *that* man to drive you right back down here. He can drop you at the door and then leave. I won't have him in this house."

"Listen to yourself, Dad. You sound irrational. The facts are that Web and I are here in Vermont for the weekend, and that when we do come by to see you, we'll be together. Now, you can shut the door on us both, but that would be very sad, because I am your daughter and I do love you."

"I'm beginning to doubt that, young lady."

It was a low blow, and one she didn't deserve after all she'd done for her parents' sake in the past fourteen years. Clenching her jaw against the anger that flared, she went on slowly and clearly. "We'll be heading back to New York tomorrow afternoon. We'll stop by at the house sometime around seven. We can talk this all out then."

"Do *not* bring *him*."

"He'll be with me, and if you refuse to see me, we'll be married by the end of the week. Think about it, Dad. I'll see you tomorrow." Without awaiting his answer, she quietly put down the phone.

Web sucked in a deep breath, then let it out in a stunned whoosh. "You are quick, lady. I never would have dreamed up that particular threat, but you've practically guaranteed that he'll see us."

"Practically," she said without pride. Then she muttered, "He *is* a bastard."

Web drew her against him. "Shhhh. He's your father, and you love him."

"For that, yes, but as a person . . ."

"Shhhh. The door's open. Let's let it go at that."

THE DOOR WAS INDEED OPEN when Marni and Web arrived Sunday evening at the handsome estate where she'd grown up. Fourteen years before, Web would have been taken aback by the splendor of the long, tree-lined drive and the majesty of the huge Georgian colonial mansion. Now he could admire it without awe or envy.

They were greeted in the front hall by Duncan, Cook's husband, who'd served as handyman, chauffeur and butler for the Langes for as long as Marni could remember. "Miss Marni, it's good to see you. You're looking fine."

"Thank you, Duncan," she said quietly. "I'd like you to meet my fiancé, Mr. Webster."

"How are you, Duncan?" Web extended his hand. He, like Marni, was unpretentious when it came to hired help. He'd always treated the most lowly of his own assistants as important members of the crew. Whereas Marni was softhearted and compassionate, Web was understanding as only one who'd once been "hired help" himself could be.

Duncan pumped his hand, clearly pleased with the offering. "Just fine, Mr. Webster. And my congratulations to you both. I had no idea we'd be having a wedding coming up here soon."

Marni cleared her throat and threw what might have been an amused glance at Web had she not been utterly incapable of amusement at that moment. "We, uh, we haven't made final plans." She paused. "My parents are expecting me, I think."

"That's right," Duncan returned with the faintest hint of tension. "They're in the library. They suggested you join them there."

The library. Warm and intimate in some homes, formal and forbidding in this one. It had been the scene of many a reprimand in Marni's youth, and that knowledge did nothing to curb her anxiety now. There were differences of course. She was no longer in her youth, and Web was with her...

Head held high, she led the way through the large front hall and down a long hallway to the room at the very end. The door was open, but the symbolism was deceptive. Marni knew what she would find even before she entered the room and nodded to her parents.

Jonathan Lange was sitting in one corner of the studded leather sofa. His legs were crossed at the knees, and one arm was thrown over the back of the sofa while the other hand held his customary glass of Scotch. He was wearing a suit, customary as well; he always wore a suit when discussing serious business.

Adele Lange sat on the sofa not far from him. She wore a simple dress, nursed an aperitif and looked eminently poised.

"Thank you for seeing us," Marni began with what she hoped was corresponding poise. "I think you remember Brian."

Neither of the Langes looked at him. "Sit down," Jonathan said stiffly, tossing his head toward one of two leather chairs opposite the sofa. That particular symbolism did have meaning, Marni mused. The two chairs were well separated by a marble coffee table.

Marni took the seat near her father, leaving the one closer to her mother for Web. She sat back, folded her hands in her lap and spoke softly. "Brian and I are planning to get married. We'd like your support."

"Why?" Jonathan asked baldly.

"Because we feel that what we're doing is right and we'd like you to share our happiness."

"Why now? It's been fourteen years since you were first involved. Fourteen years is a long time for an engagement. Why the sudden rush to marry?"

Marni was confused. "We haven't been seeing each other all that time. I hadn't seen him since the day of the accident until three weeks ago when I went to his studio to be photographed."

"But you've carried a torch for him all these years."

"No! After the accident you forbade me to see him, so I didn't. I forced myself to forget about him, to put what we had down to a seventeen-year-old's infatuation, just as you said. It wasn't a matter of carrying a torch, and I never dreamed he'd be the photographer when I stepped foot in that studio—"

"I was wondering about that, too," Jonathan interrupted scornfully. "You were in favor of this magazine thing from the start—" his eyes narrowed "—and then to suddenly come up with the photographer who just happened to be the man you'd imagined yourself in love with—"

"It wasn't that way at all!"

Web, who'd been sitting quietly, spoke for the first time. "Marni's right. She had no idea I was—"

"I'm not talking to you," Jonathan cut in, his eyes still on Marni.

Web wasn't about to be bullied. "Well, I'm talking to you, and if you have *anything* to say to me, you can look me in the eye."

Marni put out a hand. "Web, please . . ." she whispered.

He softened his tone, but that was his only concession. His eyes were sharply focused on Marni's father. "I have pictures from that first photo session, one after the other showing the shock on Marni's face. She knew nothing of the past identity of Brian Webster the photographer. No one does except your family and mine."

Though Jonathan still refused to look at him, Adele did. Instinctively Web met her gaze. "Marni hadn't been pining away for me any more than I'd been pining away for her. In hindsight I can see that she was special even back then. But it's the woman I know today whom I've fallen in love with. And it's the man I am today whom I think you should try to understand."

"There's not much to understand," Adele returned. Her voice wasn't quite as cold as her husband's had been, but it was far from encouraging. "We firmly believe that had it not been for you our son would be alive today. Can you honestly expect us to let our daughter marry you, knowing that every time we look at you we'll remember what you did?"

Web sat back. "Okay, let's get into that. Exactly what *did* I do?"

"You were recklessly driving that motorcycle," Jonathan snapped, eyes flying to Web's for the first time.

Web felt a small victory in that he'd been acknowledged as a person at last. "Is that what the police said after the investigation?"

"Ethan would never have *been* on a motorcycle had it not been for you."

"I didn't force him to get on it. He wasn't some raw kid of fourteen. He was a man of twenty-five."

"You were a bad influence that entire summer!"

"That's what you assumed, since I was only an employee at the Inn. Did Ethan ever tell you what we did together? Did he tell you that we spent hours talking politics, or philosophy, or psychology? Or that we discussed books we'd both read, or that we played chess? I loved playing chess with Ethan. I beat him three times out of four, but he took it with a grin and came back for another game more determined than ever to win. There was nothing irresponsible about what we did, and I was probably a better influence on him than the spoiled and self-centered characters he would have been with otherwise. You really should have been proud of him. He chose to be with me because the time we spent together was intellectually productive."

Marni wanted to applaud, but her fingers were too tightly intertwined to move.

Jonathan wasn't about to applaud either. Choosing to ignore what Web had said, he turned his attention back to Marni. "What were you intending with the song and dance you've been doing for the past two weeks? Did you hope to pull the wool over our eyes? Did you think we were that foolish?"

"I had hoped that you'd see Brian as he is today. Aside from his profession, which you're unfairly biased against, he's everything I'd have thought you'd want in the man I decided to marry." She turned to her mother. "What did you find out? I'm sure you made calls."

"I did," Adele sniffed. "It appears he's fooled the rest of the world, but we know him as he is."

Marni scowled. "You don't know him at all. You may have met him in passing once or twice that summer, but you never spent any time talking with him, and you certainly never invited him to the house. Don't you think it's about time you faced the fact that Ethan's death just *happened*?"

"You wouldn't say that if you were a mother, Marni. You'd be angry and grief-stricken, just like we were, like we are."

"For God's sake, it's been fourteen years!"

"Have *you* forgotten?" Adele cried.

Marni sagged in her seat. "Of course not. I adored Ethan. I'll never forget him. And I've never forgotten the sense of injustice, the anger I felt that those two cars had to collide right in Web's path. But you can't live your life feeding on anger and grief. Ethan would never have wanted it. Have you ever stopped to consider that? Web was his friend. Whether you like it or not, he was. He suffered in that accident, both physically and emotionally." She suddenly sat forward and rounded on her father. "Your response when Web called you from the hospital was *inexcusable*! How could you have done something like that? He's a human being, for God's sake, a human being!" She took a quick breath and sat straighter. "Web mourned Ethan just as we did, and he suffered through his share of guilt, though God only knows he had nothing to feel guilty for. But that's all in the past now. There's nothing any of us can do to bring Ethan back, and I refuse to live my life any longer trying to make up to you for his loss!"

"What are you talking about, girl?" Jonathan snarled.

"Marni," Web began, "you don't have to—"

"I do, Web. It's about time the entire truth came out." She faced her parents, looking from one to the other. "I felt guilty because I'd loved both Ethan and Web. Ethan was dead. Web was as good as dead to me because you never let up on the fact that he was to blame, and if he was to blame, *I* was to blame, too." She focused on her father. "Do you think I wasn't aware that you'd been grooming Ethan for the corporation presidency? And that you practically lost interest in the business after he died? Why do you think I buckled down and whipped through Wellesley, then Columbia? Didn't it ever occur to you that I was trying to be what Ethan would have been? That I felt I could somehow make things easier for you if I joined the corporation myself?" She tempered her tone, though her voice was shaky. "I'm not saying that I'd had my heart set on something else, or that I'm unhappy being where I am, but I think you should both know that what I did I did for you, even more than for me."

"Then you were a fool," was Jonathan's curt response.

"Maybe so, but I don't regret it for a minute. I did make things easier for you. You won't admit it, any more than you'll admit that I've done a good job. You never did that, Dad. Do you realize?" Her eyes had grown moist and her knuckles were white as she gripped the arms of the chair. "I tried so hard, and you promoted me and gave me more and more responsibility until finally I became president. But not once, *not once* did you tell me you were proud of me. Not once did you actually praise my work—"

Her voice cracked, and she stopped talking. She was unaware that Web had risen from his seat to stand behind hers until she felt his comforting touch on her shoulder. Her hands left the arms of the chair and found his instantly.

Jonathan's expression was as tight as ever, though his voice was quieter. "I assumed that actions spoke louder than words."

"Well, they don't! I beat my tail to the ground trying to win your approval, but I failed, I failed. And now I'm tired." Her voice reflected it. "I'm tried of trying to please someone else. I'm thirty-one years old, and it's about time I see to *my* best interests. I have every intention of continuing on as Lange's president, and I'll continue to do the best job I can, but for me now, and for Web. I'm going to marry him, and we're going to have children, and if you can't find it in your hearts to forgive, or at least forget, then I guess you'll miss out on the happiness. It's your choice. I've already made mine."

There was a moment's heavy silence in the room before Jonathan spoke in a grim voice. "I guess there's not much more to say, then, is there." It wasn't a question but a dismissal. Pushing himself from the sofa, he turned his back on them and walked toward the window.

Web addressed Adele. "There's one last thing I'd like to say," he ventured quietly. "I'd like you to consider what would have happened if Marni—or Tanya—had had Ethan for a passenger when her car crashed, killing him but only injuring her. Would you have ostracized one of your daughters from the family? Would you have held a permanent grudge? You know, that's happened in families, where two members were in an accident, one killed and the other survived. I don't know how those families reacted. Regardless of guilt or innocence, it's a tragic situation.

"Ethan and I were innocent victims of that accident fourteen years ago. Once those cars started spinning all over the road, the motorcycle didn't have a chance in hell of escaping them. If I had been the son of one of your oldest and dearest friends, would you still feel the way you do now?"

"You are *not* the son of one of our oldest and dearest friends," Jonathan said without turning. "And I thank God for it!"

MARNI AND WEB left then. They'd said what they'd come to say and had heard what they'd suspected they'd hear. They felt disappointed and saddened, hurt and angry.

"That's it, Web," Marni stated grimly as they began the drive into the city. "We know how they feel, and they're not going to change. I think we should get married, and as soon as possible."

Web kept his eyes on the road, his hands on the wheel. "Let's not do anything impulsively," he said quietly.

Her gaze flew to his face in dismay. "Impulsively? I thought marriage was what we both wanted! Weren't you the one who said that the longer we put off telling my parents the truth, the longer it would be before we got married? I thought *you* were the one who wanted to get married soon!"

"I do." His voice was even, and he didn't blink. "But we're both upset right now. It's not the ideal situation in which to be starting a marriage."

"Then what do we do? Wait forever in the hope that they'll do an about-face? They won't, Web!"

"I know. I know." He was trying to sort out his thoughts, to find some miraculous solution to their problem. "But if we rush into something, they'll be all the more perverse."

"I can't believe you're saying this! You were the one who felt so strongly that we were adults and didn't need their permission!"

He held the car steady in the right-hand lane. "We don't. And we are adults. But they're your parents, and you do love them. It'd still be nice if they came around. This all has to be a shock to them. Two days, Marni, that's all they've had."

"It wouldn't matter if it were two months!"

"It might. We presented our arguments tonight, and they were logical. I think your mother was listening, even if your father tried hard not to. Don't you think we owe them a little time to mull it over? They may never come fully around to our way of thinking, but it's possible they might decide to accept what they can't change."

Marni didn't know what to think, particularly about Web's sudden reluctance to get married. "Do you really think that could happen?" Her skepticism was nearly palpable.

"I don't know," he said with a sigh. "But I do think it's worth the wait. To rush and get married now will accomplish nothing more than throwing our relationship in their faces."

"It would accomplish much more. We'd be *married!* Or doesn't that mean as much to you as it does to me?"

"You're upset, Marni, or you wouldn't be saying that—"

"And why shouldn't we throw our relationship in their faces? We're in love. We want to get married. We asked for their support, and they refused it. They couldn't have been more blunt. I don't understand you, Web," she pleaded. "Why are you suddenly having reservations?"

He glanced at her then and saw the fear on her face. Reaching for her hand, he found it cold and stiff, so he enclosed it in his own, warmer hand and brought it to his thigh. "I'm not having reservations, sweetheart," he said gently. "Not about what I feel for you, or about getting married, or about doing all those things we've been dreaming about. If you know me at all, you know how much they mean to me. It's just that I'm trying to understand your parents, to think of what they must be feeling."

She would have tugged her hand away had he not held it firmly. "How can you be so generous after everything they've done to you?"

"Generosity has nothing to do with it," he barked. "It's selfishness from the word go."

"I don't understand."

Unable to concentrate on the road, he pulled over onto its shoulder and killed the engine. Then he turned to her and pressed her hand to his heart. "It's for *us*, Marni," he stated forcefully. "You're right. They've done a hell of a lot to me— and to you, too—and for that they don't deserve an ounce of compassion. I'd like to ignore them, to pretend they don't exist, and in the end that may be just what we'll have to do. In the meantime, though, I refuse to let them dictate any of our actions, and that includes when we'll be getting married." His voice gentled, but it maintained its urgency, and his gaze pierced Marni's through the dark of night.

"Don't you see? Our rushing to get married just because of what happened tonight would be a kind of shotgun wedding in reverse. I won't have that! We'll plan our wedding, maybe for a month or two from now, and we'll do it right. I want you wearing a beautiful gown, and I want flowers all over the place, and I want our friends there to witness the day that means so much to us. I will *not* sneak off and elope behind someone's back. I won't have our marriage tainted in any way!"

Through her upset, Marni felt a glimmer of relief. She'd begun to think that Web would put off their marriage indefinitely. A month or two she could live with. And he did have a point; the only purpose of rushing to get married in three days would be to spite her parents. "In a month or two they'll still be resisting," she warned, but less caustically.

"True, but at least we'll know that we've given them every possible chance. If we've done our best, and still they refuse to open up their minds, we'll have nothing to regret in the future." He raised her hand to his lips and gently kissed her palm. "I want it to be as perfect as it can be, sweetheart. Everything open and aboveboard. We owe that to ourselves, don't you think?"

9

DURING THE DAY following the scene with Marni's parents, Web convinced himself that he'd been right in what he'd said to Marni. Deep in his heart he suspected that her parents would never accept their marriage, and he regretted it only in terms of Marni's happiness. He had cause to think of his own, though, when he received a call from a friend on Tuesday morning.

Cole Hammond wrote for New York's most notorious gossip sheet parading as a newspaper. The two men had met in a social context soon after Web had arrived in New York, and though Web had no love for Cole's publication, he'd come to respect the man himself. When Cole asked if he could meet with Web to discuss something important, Web promptly invited him over.

"I received an anonymous call today," Cole began soon after Web had tossed him a can of beer. They were in Web's living room. The studio was still being cleaned up from the morning's shoot. "It was from a woman. She claimed that she had a sensational story about you. Something to do with an accident in Maine fourteen years ago?"

Web had had an odd premonition from the moment he'd heard Cole's voice on the phone, which was the main reason he'd had him come right over. "Yes," he agreed warily. "There was an accident."

"This woman said that you were responsible for a man's death. Any truth to it?"

Curbing his anger against "this woman" and her allegations, Web looked his friend in the eye. "No."

"She gave me dates and facts. It was a rainy night, very late, and you were speeding along on a motorcycle with a fellow named Ethan Lange on the back."

"Not speeding. But go on."

"You skidded and collided with a car. Lange was thrown and killed."

". . . Is that it?"

"She said you'd been drinking that night and that you had no business being on the road."

"What else?"

Cole shrugged. "That's it. I thought I'd run it by you before I did anything more with it."

"I'm glad you have, for your sake more than mine." Web's entire body was rigid with barely leashed fury. "If you're hoping to get a story out of this, I'd think twice. In the first place, she had the facts wrong. In the second place, the police report will bear that out. And in the third place, if you print something like this, you'll have a hefty lawsuit on your hands. I will not stand by and let you—"

"Hold on, pal," Cole interrupted gently, raising a hand, palm out. "I'd never print a thing without getting the facts straight, which is why I'm here. I know you don't trust the paper, but this is *me*. We've talked about situations like this many times. If the facts don't merit a story, there won't *be* a story." He sat back. "So. Why don't you tell me what happened that night?"

Web took a deep breath and forced himself to calm down. Very slowly and distinctly, he outlined the facts of the accident. By the time he was done, he was back on the edge of fury. "You're being used, Cole. I don't know who the caller was, but I've got a damned good idea.... Is this off the record now, just between us?"

"We're friends. Of course it is."

Web trusted him. He also knew that nothing he was about to say wouldn't come out eventually, and that if Cole chose to print it, friend or no, Web would have even greater grounds for a lawsuit. He knew that Cole knew it, too.

"I'm engaged to marry Marni Lange. It was her brother who died that night. Her parents have always blamed me for the accident, regardless of the facts or the police report. Needless to say, they're totally against our marriage. I suspect that it was her sister who called you, and that her major purpose was vengeance."

Cole ingested the possibility thoughtfully. "It's not a unique motive."

"You should be livid."

The other shrugged. "One out of four may be done for vengeance, but even then there's often a story that will sell."

"Well, there isn't one here. It's history. It may be tragic, but it's not spectacular. Hey, go ahead and check out my story. Get that police report. You can even interview the drivers of the other two cars. They were the first ones to say that there wasn't anything I could have done, that both of them had passed me on the road right before the accident, and that I wasn't weaving around or driving recklessly. The bartender at the tavern we'd been to said we'd been stone sober when we'd left. The first car skidded. The second one collided with it and started spinning. I braked, but the road was wet. I might even have been able to steer clear if one of those cars hadn't careened into me." He took a quick breath, then sagged. "It's all there in black and white. An old story. Not worth fiddling with."

"If you were a nobody, I'd agree with you." When Web bolted forward, he held up his hand again. "Listen, what you say makes sense. I'm just doing my job."

"Your job sucks. This isn't *news*, for God's sake!"

"I agree."

"Do you trust me?"

"I always have."

"Do you believe that what I've told you is the truth?"

Cole paused. "Yes, I believe you."

"Then . . . you'll forget you got that call?"

Another pause, then a nod. "I will." And a sly grin. "But will you?"

"Not on your life! Someone's going to answer for it!"

"Watch what you do," Cole teased. "You may give me a story yet. Though come to think of it, you've got my news editor wrapped around your little finger. I'm not sure she could bear to print anything adverse about you."

Web's answering grin was thin and dry. "If it'd sell, she'd do it. . . . Give her a kiss for me, will you?"

"My pleasure."

MARNI'S GUESS AS TO WHO the caller had been matched Web's, and her anger was as volatile as his had initially been. Fortunately he'd had time to calm down.

"Tanya! That bitch! How could she *dare* try to pull something like this?"

Web put his arm around her and spoke gently. "Maybe she's trying to score points with your parents."

"She's starting at zero, so it won't get her very far," Marni scoffed, then her voice rose. "Maybe my parents put her up to it!"

"Nah. I don't think so, and you shouldn't either, sweetheart. They wouldn't sink that low, would they? I mean, voicing their disapproval to us is one thing, dirty tricks another. And besides, if the whole story came out, particularly the part about our relationship, they'd be as embarrassed as anyone. They wouldn't knowingly hurt themselves."

"I'm not sure 'knowingly' has anything to do with it. They seem to be incapable of rational thought. That's the problem." She pulled away from Web and reached for the phone. "I'm calling Tanya."

His hand settled over hers, preventing further movement. "No. Don't do it."

"She may contact another paper. For that matter, how do we know she hasn't already?"

"Because Cole's is the sleaziest. It's the only one that would have considered touching the story. I'm sure she knew that."

Marni marveled at Web's composure. "Aren't you angry?"

"This morning I would have willingly rung Tanya's neck if I'd seen her. But that wouldn't accomplish anything. It's over, Marni. Cole won't write any story, and confronting Tanya will only make her more determined to do something else."

"What else could she do?" Marni asked with a hysterical laugh.

AS IT HAPPENED, it wasn't Tanya, but Marni's father who had something else in mind. The first Marni got wind of it was in a phone call she received on Wednesday afternoon from one of the corporation's directors. He was an old family friend, which eased Marni's indignation somewhat when he suggested that her father was disturbed about her relationship with Brian Webster, and that he hoped she wasn't making a mistake. She calmly assured him that she wasn't, and that no possible harm could come to the corporation from her marriage to Web.

The second call, though, wasn't as excusable. It came on Thursday morning and was from another of the directors. This one was not a family friend and therefore, theoretically, had no cause to question her private life. Livid, she hung up the phone after talking with him, then stewed at her desk for a time, trying to decide on the best course of action. Indeed, action was called for. If her father was planning to undermine her authority by individually calling each member of the board, she wasn't about to take it sitting down.

She promptly instructed her administrative assistant to summon the board members for a meeting the following morning.

"Your father, too?" Web asked incredulously when she called him to tell him what had happened.

"Yes, my father, too. You were right. Everything should be open and aboveboard. He can hear what I'm going to say along with everyone else."

"What *are* you going to say?"

Her voice dropped for the first time. "I'm not sure." With the next breath, her belligerency resurfaced. "But I'm taking the offensive. Dad's obviously been planting seeds of doubt about me. The only thing I can do is nip it in the bud." She paused, knowing that for all the conviction she might project, she'd called Web because she desperately needed his support.

He didn't let her down. "I agree, sweetheart. I think you've made the right decision. One thing I've learned from talking with you about the corporation is that you haven't gotten where you are by sitting back and waiting for things to happen. You're doing the right thing, Marni. I know it."

She sighed. "I hope so. If Dad has an argument with what I say, he can voice it before the board. Maybe *they* can talk some sense into him."

"Will they?" Web asked very softly. "Will they stand up for you instead of him? How strong is his hold over them?"

"I'll know soon enough, won't I?" she asked sadly.

MARNI STAYED LATE at the office, working with her administrative assistant and secretary to gather, copy and assemble for distribution an armada of facts, figures and reports.

She spent the night with Web at his place, but a pall hung over them, one they couldn't begin to shake. They both sensed that the outcome of Marni's meeting would be telling in terms of her future with the corporation. While on the one hand it was absurd to think that she'd be ousted simply because she married Web, on the other hand neither of them had dreamed Jonathan Lange would do what he already had.

"And if it happens, sweetheart?" Web asked. They were lying quietly curled against each other in bed. Sleep eluded them completely. "What if they side with your father? What will you do then?"

She'd thought about that. "My choice has been made, Web. I told you that. I love you. Our future together is the most important thing to me."

"But you love your work—"

"And I have no intention of giving it up. If the board goes against me, I'll submit my resignation and look for another position. Corporate executives often jump around. We keep the headhunters in business."

"Would you be happy anywhere else but at Lange?"

She smiled up at him, very sure about what she was going to say. "If it meant that I could have both you and my own peace of mind, I'd be happy. Yes, I'd be happy."

AT TEN O'CLOCK the following morning, Marni entered the boardroom. She'd chosen to wear a sedate white wool suit with a navy blouse and accessories. Her hair was perfect, as was her makeup. She knew that no one in the room could fault her appearance. She represented Lange well.

Twelve of the fourteen members of the board were present, talking quietly among themselves until she took her seat at one end of the long table. Her father was at the other. He stood stiffly, and the room was suddenly quiet.

"I will formally call this meeting to order, but since my daughter was the one who organized it, and since I am myself in the dark as to its purpose, I will turn it over to her."

Ignoring both his glower and his very obvious impatience, Marni stood. She rested her hands lightly on the alternating stacks of papers that had been set there for her by her assistant. "Thank you all for coming," she said with quiet confidence, looking from one face to the next, making eye contact wherever possible. "I appreciate the fact that many of you have had to cancel other appointments on such short notice, but I felt the urgency was called for." Pausing, she lifted the first pile of papers from the stack, divided it and sent one half down each side of the table. "Please help yourselves. These are advance copies of our latest production figures, division by division, subsidiary by subsidiary. I don't expect you to read through them now, but I think when you do you'll see that the last quarter was the most productive one Lange has had to date. We're growing, ladies and gentlemen, and we're healthy."

She went to the next pile of papers and passed them around in like fashion. "These are proposals for projects we hope to launch within the next few months. Again, read them at your leisure. I believe that you'll find them exciting, and that you'll see the potential profit in each." She waited until the last of the papers had been distributed, using the time to bolster herself for the tougher part to come. When she had the attention of all those present once more, she went on quietly.

"It is important to me that the board knows of everything that is happening at Lange, and since I'm it's president, and as such more visible than our other employees, I want you to be informed and up-to-date on what is happening to me personally." As she spoke her gaze skipped from one member to the next, though she studiously avoided her father's face. He would either intimidate or infuriate her, she feared, and in any case would jeopardize her composure.

"At some point within the next two months, I'll be getting married. My fiancé's name is Brian Webster. Perhaps some of you have heard of him. If not, you'll read about him in the papers I've given you. He's been chosen as the cover photographer for *Class*, the new magazine our publishing division will be putting out. Let me say now that, although Mr. Webster and I knew each other many years ago, the decision to hire him was made first and foremost by the publishing division. At the time I didn't realize that the man I knew so long ago was the same photographer New York has gone wild for. We met, and I realized who he was only after the contracts had been signed and he'd begun to work for us."

There were several nods of understanding from various members of the group, so she went on. "The fact of my marriage will in no way interfere with the quality of work

I do for Lange. I believe you all know of my dedication to the corporation. Mr. Webster certainly knows of it. My father built this business from scratch, and I take great pride in seeing that it grows and prospers." She dared a glance at her father then. He was sitting straight, his eyes hard, his lips compressed into a thin line. She quickly averted her gaze to more sympathetic members of the group.

"You may be asking yourself why I felt it so important to call you here simply to tell you of my engagement. I did it because I wanted to assure you that I intend to continue as president of Lange. But there was another reason as well. There is," she said slowly, "a very important matter concerning Brian Webster and my family that some of you may already know about, but which I wanted all of you to hear about first hand. There is apt to be speculation, and perhaps some ill will, but I'm counting on you all to keep that in perspective."

She lifted her hand from the last pile of papers and sent them around the table. "Fourteen years ago Brian Webster and my brother Ethan were good friends. Brian was the one driving the motorcycle on the night Ethan was killed."

Barely a murmur surfaced among those present, which more than anything told Marni that her father had been busier than she'd thought. The knowledge made her all the more determined to thwart his efforts to discredit both her and Web.

"What you have before you are copies of the police report from that night. You'll learn that Mr. Webster was found entirely without fault in the accident. I've also included excerpts from articles about Brian and his work. They were gathered by the publishing division when it cast its vote for him as the *Class* photographer. I don't think any of us can fault either his qualifications or his character."

She took a deep breath and squared her shoulders. "There are some who will claim that Brian was responsible for Ethan's death, and that I am therefore acting irresponsibly by thinking of marrying him. Once you've read what I've given you, I feel confident that you'll agree with me that this is not the case. In no way could Brian Webster embarrass this corporation, or me, and in no way could he adversely affect the job I plan to do as your continuing president."

She looked down, moistened her lips, then raised her chin high. "Are there any questions I might answer? If any of you have doubts as to my moral standing, I'd appreciate your airing them now." Her gaze passed from one director to another. There were shrugs, several headshakes, several frighteningly bland expressions. And then there was her father.

With both hands on the edge of the table, he pushed himself to his feet. "I have questions, and doubts, but you've already heard them."

"That's right. I have. I'd like to know if any of the other members of the board share your opinion. If a majority of the others agree with you, I'll submit my resignation as of now and seek a position elsewhere."

That statement did cause a minor stir, but it consisted of gasps and grunts, the swiveling of heads and a shifting in seats, so that in the end Marni wasn't sure whether the group was in her favor or against. Her gaze encompassed all those who would sit in judgment on her.

"I truly believe that what we have here is a difference of opinion between my father and myself." She purposely didn't include mention of her mother or Tanya. "It should have remained private, and would have, had it not been for calls that were made to several of you that I know of, perhaps all of you—which is why I've asked you here today. It's not your place to decide who I should or shouldn't marry, but since it is in your power to decide whether or not I remain as president of this corporation, I felt that my interests, and Brian's, should be represented.

"As it is, someone tried to plant a story in one of the local papers." She was staring at her father then and was oblivious to the other eyes that widened in dismay. "It would have been a scandal based on nothing but sleazy headlines. Fortunately, Brian is well enough respected in this community that the writer who received the anonymous tip very quickly dismissed it as soon as he heard the truth. Now—" her eyes circled the room again "—do any of you have questions I can answer before I leave?"

Emma Landry spoke up, smiling. "When's the wedding?"

Marni smiled in return. She knew she had one ally. "We haven't set the date yet."

"Will we all be invited?" asked Geoffrey Gould.

"Every one of you," she said, seeking out her father's gaze and holding it for a minute before returning her attention to the group. There were several stern faces among them, several more meek. All she could do was to pray she'd presented her case well.

"If there are no further questions," she said, taking a breath, "I'll leave you to vote on whether I'll be staying on as president. If you say 'yes,' I'll take it as a vote of confidence in what I've done at Lange during the past seven years. If you say 'no,' I'll accept it with regret and move on." Her voice lowered and was for the first time less steady as she looked at her father a final time. "I'll be at my mother's awaiting your decision."

That, too, had been a studied decision. Marni had felt that it would be a show, albeit false, of some support from her family. But she did want to tell Adele what she'd done. If she failed with this group, her mother would witness firsthand her pain. If she succeeded, it would be a perfect opportunity to try to swing Adele to her way of thinking.

Marni had no idea that Web was a full step ahead of her.

"I APPRECIATE YOUR SEEING ME, Mrs. Lange," Web said after he was shown into the solarium at the back of the house. "I would have called beforehand, but I didn't want to be turned down on the phone. I know that your husband is in the city at a meeting of the board of directors."

"That's right," Adele said quietly. She was sitting in a high-backed wicker chair, with her elbows on its broad arms and her hands resting in her lap.

"You're probably wondering why I'm here, and, to tell you the truth—" he rubbed the tense muscles at the back of his neck "—part of me is, too. It was obvious at our last meeting that you agree with your husband in your opinion of me, and I'm not sure I could change it if I wanted to." He sighed and sat forward, propping his elbows on his thighs. He studied his hands, which hung between his knees, then frowned.

"Perhaps this is a sexist thing to say, but I thought I might appeal to your softer side. All women have a softer side. I know Marni does. Right about now it's not showing, because she's addressing the board of directors, and I'm sure she's making as businesslike a pitch as she can for their understanding. But the softer side's there, not very far from the surface. Marni loves me. She's aching because she loves you both, too, and it hurts her that she's had to make a choice between us."

"She chose you," Adele stated evenly. "I'd think you would be pleased."

He looked up. "Pleased, yes. I'm pleased, and relieved, because I don't think I could make it through a future without her. But I don't feel a sense of victory, if that's what you're suggesting. There's no victory when a family is torn apart, particularly one that has already suffered its share of loss."

Adele arched a brow. "Do *you* know about loss, Mr. Webster?"

"No. At least, not as you know it. One can't lose things one has never had. I never had a father. Did you know that?"

"No. No, I didn't."

"There's a lot you don't know about me. I'd like to tell you, if I may."

Adele paused, then nodded. Though she maintained an outer semblance of arrogance, there was a hint of curiosity in her eyes. Web wasn't about to pass that up.

"I never knew my father. He and my mother didn't marry. When I was two my mother married another man, a good man, a hard worker. I'm afraid I didn't make things terribly easy for him. For reasons I didn't understand at the time, I was restless. I hated school, but I loved to learn. I spent my nights reading everything I could get my hands on, but during the days I felt compelled to move around. Instead of going to college, I took odd jobs where I could find them. I traveled the world, literally, working my way from one place to the next.

"Then I met Ethan. We shared a mutual respect. Through him, I realized I had to settle down, that I wouldn't get anywhere if I didn't focus in on one thing and try to be good at it. I was a jack of all trades, master of none. And I was tired of it."

He gazed at his thumbnail, pressed it with his other thumb. "Maybe I'd simply reached an age where it was time to grow up. After Ethan died, I did a lot of thinking. There were many unresolved feelings I had, about my father and about myself. I don't know who my father is, so those feelings will remain unresolved to a point. But fourteen years ago I realized that I couldn't let them affect my life, that I didn't really need to be running around to escape that lack of identity. That if I stayed in one place and built a life, a reputation for myself, I could make up for it."

He raised his eyes to Adele's intent ones and wondered if she realized the extent of her involvement with his story. "I think I have. But there's more I want, and it involves Marni." He sat up in the chair. "I adore that woman, Mrs. Lange. You have no idea how much. I want to marry her, and we want children."

"You've already told us that," Adele pointed out, but the edge was gone from her voice.

"Yes, but I'm not sure if you realize how much Marni wants our family to encompass you and your husband. Do you want her to be happy, Mrs. Lange?"

"Of course. I'm her mother. What mother wouldn't want that for her daughter?"

"I don't know," he said slowly. "That's what I'm trying to understand."

"Are you accusing me of being blind to what Marni needs, when she sat here herself last Sunday night and announced that she'd go ahead with her plans regardless of what we said or did?"

He kept his tone gentle. "I'm not accusing you of anything. What I'm suggesting is that maybe you don't fully understand Marni's needs. I'm not sure I did myself until I heard what she said to you the other night. She badly wants your approval. You're right, she and I will go ahead and get married even if you continue to hold out. We'll have our home and our children, and we'll be happy. But there will always be a tiny part of Marni that will feel the loss of her parents, and it will be such a premature and unnecessary loss that it will be all the sadder." He paused. "How will *you* feel about such a loss? You lost your son through a tragedy none of us could control. This one would be a tragedy of your own making."

"Ethan would have been alive if it hadn't been—"

"Do you honestly believe that? *Honestly?* Am I a killer, Mrs. Lange? Look at me and tell me if you think I am truly a killer."

Scowling, she shifted in her seat. "Well, not in the sense of a hardened criminal . . ."

"Not in any sense. I think in your heart you agree. Otherwise you never would have let me talk with you today."

"My husband's out. That's why I'm talking with you today."

"Then he's the one who dictates your opinion?"

"We've been married for nearly forty years, Mr. Webster. I respect what my husband feels strongly about."

"Even when he's wrong?"

"I . . . I owe him my loyalty."

"But what about the loyalty you owe your children? You had a choice when it came to picking your husband. Your children had no choice about being born. You gave them life and brought them into this world. They had no say in the matter. Marni didn't *choose* you to be her mother, any more than she chose to be Ethan's sister. And she didn't choose to have him killed in that accident, yet she's spent the past fourteen years trying to make up to you for it. Don't you owe her some kind of loyalty for that?"

"Now you're asking me to make a choice between my daughter and my husband."

"No. I'm simply asking you to decide for yourself whether Marni's marrying me would be so terrible, and if you decide that it wouldn't be, that you try to convince your husband of it. We're not asking for an open-armed welcome. We'll very happily settle for peaceful coexistence. You don't have to love me, Mrs. Lange, but if you love your daughter you'll respect the fact that *she* loves me."

"Web!"

Both heads in the room riveted toward its door, where Marni was standing in a state of utter confusion. Web came instantly to his feet.

"What are you doing here?" she asked, her brows knitting as she looked from him to her mother and back.

"We were just talking." He approached her quickly, ran his hands along her arms and spoke very softly. "How did it go?"

"I don't know. I left before they took a vote. Then I needed a little time to myself, so I took the roundabout way getting here." Apprehension was written all over her face. "There's been no word?"

Web hesitated, then shook his head.

Adele frowned. "A vote? What vote?"

"As to whether I should remain as president. I tendered my resignation, pending the board's decision."

Adele, too, was on her feet then. "You didn't! What a foolish thing to do, Marni! You've been a fine president! You can't be replaced!"

"Oh, I can. No one's indispensable."

"But we always intended that the presidency should remain in the family!"

"Maybe Tanya should give it a try," Marni suggested dryly, only to be answered by an atypical and distinctly unladylike snort from her mother.

"Tanya! That's quite amusing." Her head shot up. "Jonathan! When did *you* get here?"

Web had seen the man approach, but Marni, with her back to the door, had had no such warning. Turning abruptly, her heart in her throat, she faced the tired and stern face of her father.

10

AT ONE TIME Marni might have run to Jonathan Lange. Too much had passed between them in recent days, though, and she grew rigid as he approached. Web dropped his hands to his sides but stayed close, offering his silent support as they both waited to hear what her father had to say.

The older man ran a hand through his thinning gray hair, then glanced at his wife. "I could use a drink."

"Duncan? Duncan!" Adele's voice rang out, and the butler promptly appeared. "Mr. Lange will have his usual. I'll have mine with water." She turned to Marni and Web, her brows raised. When they both shook their heads, she nodded to Duncan. "That will be all."

Jonathan walked past them, deeper into the solarium. He stopped before one glass expanse, thrust his hands in his pockets and, stiff-backed, stood with his feet apart as he gazed at the late March landscape.

Marni stared after him. She knew he had news, but whether it was good or bad she had no idea. In that instant she realized how very much she did want to stay on as president of Lange.

Adele looked from Marni to her husband, then back.

Web, standing close behind Marni, put his hands lightly at her waist. "Do you want to sit down?" he asked softly.

She shook her head, but her eyes didn't leave her father's rigid back. "Dad? What happened?"

Jonathan didn't answer immediately. He raised a hand and scratched his neck, then returned the hand to his pocket. Duncan entered the solarium, offered Adele her drink from a small silver tray, then crossed the room to offer Jonathan his. Only when the butler had left did Jonathan turn. He held the drink in both hands, watching his thumbs as they brushed against the condensation beginning to form on the side of the glass.

"I didn't know she'd done that, Marni," he began solemnly. "I had no idea Tanya had called that reporter—"

"What reporter?" Adele interrupted fearfully. "What has Tanya done?"

There was sadness, almost defeat in the expression Jonathan turned on his wife. "Tanya tried to plant a story in the newspaper about the accident and Webster's role in it."

Adele clutched her glass to her chest. "Tanya did *that*?"

Jonathan's gaze met Marni's. "I have no proof that it was Tanya, but no one else would have had cause except perhaps your mother and I. But I never would have condoned something like that. I'll have a thing or two to say to your sister when I call her later."

Marni couldn't move. Her heart was pounding as she waited, waited. "It's not important. What happened at the meeting? Was a vote taken?"

He took a drink. The ice rattled as he lowered his glass "Yes."

"And . . . ?"

Jonathan studied the ice, but it was Marni who felt its chill. "You'll be staying on as president of Lange. There was an easy majority in your favor."

Marni closed her eyes in a moment's prayerful thanks. Web's hands tightened on her waist when she swayed. It was his support, and the warmth of his body reaching out to her, that gave her the strength to open her eyes and address her father again.

"And you, Dad? How did you vote?"

Jonathan cleared his throat. "I exercised my right to abstain."

It was better than a flat-out 'no,' but it left major questions unanswered. "May I ask why?"

He tipped his head fractionally in a gesture of acquiescence. "I felt that I was too emotionally involved to make a rational decision."

"Then you do question my ability as president?"

He cleared his throat again. As before, it brought him an extra few seconds to formulate his response. "No. I simply question my own ability to see the truth one way or the other."

Such a simple statement, Marni mused, yet it was a powerful concession. Up to that point, Jonathan had refused to see anything but what he wanted to see. The fact that he could admit his view might be jaded was a major victory.

Web felt the release of tension in Marni's body. He, too, had immediately understood the significance of Jonathan's statement, and he shared her relief and that small sense of triumph, even hope. Lowering his head, he murmured, "Perhaps we should leave your parents alone now. I think both you and your father have been through enough today."

She knew he was right. It was a matter of quitting while she was ahead. If she stayed and forced her father to say more, she might well push him into a corner. He was a proud man. For the present it was enough to leave with the hope that one day he might actually join her in *her* corner.

Mutely she nodded. Under Web's guiding hand, she left the solarium and walked back through the house to the front door. Only when she reached it did she realize that her mother had come along.

"Darling..." Adele began. Her hand clutched the doorknob, and she seemed unsure of herself. Marni had turned, surprised and slightly wary. "I...I'm pleased things worked out for you with the board."

"So am I," Marni answered quietly. "I never really wanted to leave Lange."

Adele's voice was a whisper. "I know that." She gave an awkward smile, reached up as if to stroke Marni's hair, but drew her hand back short of physical contact. "Perhaps...perhaps we can get together for lunch one day next week?"

Marni wasn't about to look a gift horse in the mouth. She was pleased, and touched. "I'd like that, Mom. Will you call?"

Adele nodded, her eyes suspiciously moist. She did touch Marni then, wrapping an arm around her waist and pressing a cheek to hers in a quick hug. "You'd better leave now," she whispered. "Drive safely."

Marni, too, felt the emotion of the moment. She nodded and smiled through her own mist of tears, then let Web guide her out the door and down the front steps to their cars.

"I DON'T BELIEVE THESE!" Marni exclaimed in delight. She was sitting cross-legged on Web's bed, wearing nothing but the stack of photographs he'd so nonchalantly tossed into her lap moments before. "They're incredible!"

He came to sit behind her, fitting his larger body to hers so that he could look over her shoulder at the pictures he'd taken three days before. "They're *you*. Exactly what I wanted for the premier cover of *Class*."

Astonished, Marni flipped from one shot to the next. "They're all so good, Web! How are you ever going to decide which one to use? For that matter, how did you ever get so many perfect ones?"

He nipped at her bare shoulder, then soothed the spot with his chin. "I had a super model. That's all there is to it. As for which one to use, I've got my personal preference, but your people will have some say in that." He curled one long arm around hers and extracted a print from the pile. "I sent a duplicate of this one to your parents yesterday."

She met his gaze at her shoulder. "You didn't."

"I did. It's beautiful, don't you think? Every parent should have a picture like this of his daughter."

"But...isn't that a little heavy-handed? I mean, Mom and I have just begun to talk things through." Two weeks had passed since the board meeting, and she'd met with her mother as many times during that stretch.

"You said yourself that she's softening up. And if anything will speed up the process, this will. Look at it, Marni. Look at your expression here. It's so...*you*. The determined set of chin, the little bit of mischief at the mouth, the tilt of the eyebrows with just a hint of indignation, and the eyes, ah, the eyes..."

"Filled with love," she whispered, but she wasn't looking at the picture. Her own eyes were reflected in Web's, and the love flowing between them was awesome.

Web caught his breath, then haphazardly scattered the pictures from Marni's lap and turned her so she was straddling his legs. His fingers delved into her hair, and he held her face steady. "I love you, sunshine. Ohhh, do I love you." When she smiled, he ran his tongue over the curve. Then he caught her lower lip between his own lips and sipped at it.

Marni was floating wild and free, with Web as her anchor, the only one she'd ever truly need. She slipped her arms around his neck and tangled her fingers in the hair at his nape, fighting for his lips, then his tongue, then the very air he breathed.

"Where did you ever...get that passion?" he gasped. His hands had begun a questing journey over the planes and swells of her soft body.

"From you, my dear man," she breathed, greedily bunching her fingers over the twisting muscles of his back. "You taught me...fourteen years ago...and I haven't been the same since...ahhh, Web..." He'd found her breasts and was taunting them mercilessly. "Will it always...be this way?"

"Always." He rolled her nipples between his thumb and forefinger and was rewarded by her gasp.

"Promise?" She spread her hand over his flat middle and let it follow the tapering line of dark hair to that point where it flared.

"Sunshine...mmmmmmm...ah, yesss..." What little thought her artful stroking left him was centered in his fingers, which found the tiny nub of pleasure between her legs and began to caress it as artfully. "Ahhhh, sweet...so moist, soft..."

They were both breathing shallowly, and Marni's body had begun to quiver in tune with his.

"C'mere," he ordered. Cupping her bottom, he drew her forward, capturing her mouth and swallowing her rapturous moan as he entered her.

Knees braced on either side of his hips, she moved in rhythm with him. Her breasts rubbed against his with each forward surge, and their mouths mated hungrily. They rose together on passion's ladder, reaching the very highest rung before Web held her back.

"Watch," he whispered. He lowered his gaze to the point of their joining, then, when her head too was bowed, he slowly withdrew, as slowly filled her again, then repeated the movement.

It was too much for Marni. She cried his name once, then threw back her head and closed her eyes tight upon the waves of pulsing sensation that poured through her.

Web held himself buried deep inside her, hoping to savor each one of her spasms, but their very strength was his undoing. Without so much as another thrust, he gave a throaty moan and exploded. Arms trembling, he clutched her tightly to him. She was his anchor in far more than the storm of passion. He could only thank God that she was his.

ON A BRIGHT, SUNNY MORNING in early June, Marni and Web were married. The ceremony was held beneath the trees in the backyard of the Langes' Long Island estate and was followed by a lavish lawn luncheon for the two hundred invited guests.

Marni's mother was radiant, exuding the air of confidence that was her social trademark. Marni's father was gracious, if stoical, accepting congratulations with the formality that was his professional trademark.

Marni was in seventh heaven. Her mother had been the one to insist that the wedding be held there, and she'd personally orchestrated every step of the affair. While her father hadn't once vocally blessed the marriage, Marni had seen the tears in his eyes in those poignant moments when he'd led her down the rose-strewn aisle and to the altar, then given her away. She'd whispered a soft "I love you" to him as she'd kissed him, but after that her eyes had been only for Web.

"I now pronounce you man and wife," the minister had said, and she'd gone into Web's arms with a sense of joy, of fulfillment and promise that had once only been a dream.

In the years to come, they'd have their home, their careers and their children. Most important, though, they'd have each other. Their ties went back to when they'd both been young. They'd weathered personal storms along the way, but they'd emerged as better people, and their love was supreme.

Harlequin Temptation

COMING NEXT MONTH

#117 A PERMANENT ARRANGEMENT
Jane Silverwood

Ben Gallagher brought new meaning to the words "love thy neighbor." One week after moving in across the street, the sexy bachelor was making moves on Paula.

#118 DIAMOND IN THE ROUGH
Helen Conrad

Cal James was just the man Marlo Santee needed for her latest ad campaign. And she knew just the way to rope him into doing it!

#119 SERENDIPITY Judith McWilliams

What does the theft of a small white mouse have to do with a famous research scientist pursuing one of the cleaning staff? Find out in the madcap yet steamy romantic romp of Ann and Marcus.

#120 BY INVITATION ONLY
Lorena McCourtney

Most reluctantly Shar agreed to test the fidelity of her best friend's man . . . via seduction. But when she discovered she wanted Tal O'Neil all to herself, her loyalty was on the line. . . .

ATTRACTIVE, SPACE SAVING BOOK RACK

Display your most prized novels on this handsome and sturdy book rack. The hand-rubbed walnut finish will blend into your library decor with quiet elegance, providing a practical organizer for your favorite hard-or soft-covered books.

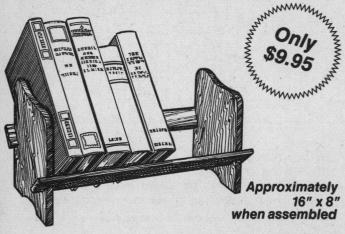

Only $9.95

Approximately 16" x 8" when assembled

Assembles in seconds!

To order, rush your name, address and zip code, along with a check or money order for $10.70 ($9.95 plus 75¢ postage and handling) (New York residents add appropriate sales tax), payable to *Harlequin Reader Service* to:

In the U.S.

Harlequin Reader Service
Book Rack Offer
901 Fuhrmann Blvd.
P.O. Box 1325
Buffalo, NY 14269-1325

Offer not available in Canada.

BKR-1

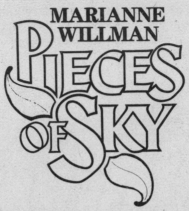
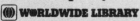